# THE OTHER SIDE OF THE VELVET ROPE

*A Novel*

*Dwight BoNey*

Copyright © 2017 Dwight BoNey
Like Water Publishing LLC. All rights reserved.

ISBN-10:0692743987
ISBN-13: 9780692743980
Library of Congress Control Number: 2016910357
Dwight BoNey, Townsend, DE

# PREFACE

The club is a place where you can sweat out the frustrations associated with the inequities of life. The club takes the guy who washes the lettuce at the local fast-food establishment and transforms him into Tony Manero from *Saturday Night Fever*. Music videos depict the club's atmosphere as euphoric, with the most beautiful women wearing as little clothing as possible. These voluptuous vixens swarm in abundance like bees to honey. The scene is like a modern-day Greek orgy with music; partially naked, inebriated partiers; and of course, fondling of various extremities. The lights are bright and flashing, as if emulating the scene of a traffic stop at nightfall. Everything is in slow motion as the coolest of the cool glide across the floor. Men stroll across the vast dance floor as if unaware of the most glamorous women flailing, thrusting, and contorting their bodies in a rhythmic pattern that makes their breasts and butts move hypnotically back and forth. This is the way the world wants you to envision the nightlife. Everyone is attractive, young, and of course, rich enough to make it rain.

Many are convinced it is a glamorous place for social interaction. Truthfully, it is a den of immorality. In some ways, the club is reminiscent of the hell described by Dante Alighieri's *Divine Comedy*, with the dance floor being the frozen lake trapping the most treacherous of society for all eternity. Some of these individuals spend countless nights betraying others for their own capital gain or simply for amusement. This is the dark, insidious place I remember. The women wear their fuck-me dresses, a one-piece garment tight enough to make their thimble-like nipples almost pierce the elastic fabric that restricts them from full disclosure. The rest of the costume clings for dear life around every curvature, like a rock climber with a death grip on the side of a mountain. The fabric draped tightly around the curvaceous posterior is just enough to cover it. Unlike the women in music videos; these women are not models. There are no bottles of champagne popping like firecrackers on the Fourth of July. Instead, they take a few leftover pieces of change from their laundry stash, which tallies to a meager three or four dollars of nickels, dimes, and pennies, to purchase dollar drinks. Some choose to drink and use drugs to drown out reality while playing out their imaginary role of a star. This combination can reduce every inhibition, inviting additional vices to take control. The inebriated become the prey of the wolves lurking in the dimness surrounding the dance floor. In the shadows, only glowing eyes are visible in the darkness: watching like those of animals lurking in the foliage, salivating and waiting for the moment when they can pounce.

Then suddenly the loudspeaker amplifies the last call for drinks, followed by the last song of the night. The blackened room lights up as if morning has come early, and all the ghouls of the night scurry for the exit to return to darkness. The security staff ushers out the stragglers while the bartenders close the last of the tabs. The owners survey the area to estimate how much needs to be cleaned from the colorful drinks that have spilled on the floor. They ponder how many glasses have been broken. Last, they quickly assess the floor, searching for those scattered puddles of vomit that occasionally arise when the darkness lifts.

The time is about 1:30 a.m., and by now, people cover the parking lot. They are walking and conversing. The scene resembles an outdoor street festival. The staff do their best to get the patrons in their cars so they will leave without incident. Cars drive by, slowly scanning for familiar faces or just looking for trouble. A vehicle with a woman driver, a woman in the passenger's seat, and a toddler with pigtails sitting on the lap of a woman with a stern face in the backseat—it's obvious they are looking for an absent father on the prowl. Other ladies have dashed between cars to squat and urinate without falling over from the imbalance associated with a drunken equilibrium.

For the hunters and the hunted, the night isn't over. This is the time for the fastest of the fast to woo their vulnerable prey. One victim, unaware of the suitor's positive AIDS test, is persuaded to spend one life-changing night with a new acquaintance. This occurs while the street-corner pharmacist makes one last transaction to the dependent user constantly searching for the perfect high to eliminate all emotional trauma. These events occur concurrently and on occasion will come to a rapid stop because two groups erupt in a verbal confrontation. This oral altercation quickly escalates to punches and ultimately reaches its apex with the echoing crackling sound of a gun—*bang!* The crowd immediately disperses.

Welcome to the other side of the velvet rope.

# CHAPTER 1
# SOLEMNITY

I can't stand looking at pictures of Anthony in that oak box, his lifeless body lying there on a white satin interior with his eyes closed and his glasses on. What a ridiculous concept. Why put glasses on him? It's not like he needs them. I assumed the spectacles gave those left behind a familiar image of someone they have lost. Still, it made my stomach do somersaults seeing him like that, all stiff and pale, dressed in his Sunday best. That's why I didn't attend Anthony's burial.

It's 2016, and I am still looking at these pictures from six years ago my longtime friend Dominic gave me. Who could imagine that this would be the first of three unexpected tragedies? I never liked funerals. I wanted to remember people how they were when they were alive. On the day of Anthony's funeral, I knew I wouldn't be able to overcome my dislike of these events. I couldn't bear to see the lifeless image of him in his new, upholstered tomb. He was only thirty-two when he passed. That's just two years older than I was at the time of his death.

We used to go to the gym daily to stay in shape and go out drinking every night we were off from the club. By the time of his death, those days had all come to pass. It's hard to fathom that we will never take a shot of Grand Marnier, or GM, as we called it, ever again. Our careers had started to take shape, and working at the club was over. We had finally grown up, gotten married, and had baby boys born within months of each other. Oddly, the last correspondence between us came by way of e-mailed pictures of our baby boys in the hospital right after being born. I never deleted those e-mails, and still to this day, I will take a moment to glance at them while reminiscing. The smiles on our faces in those photos were larger than life. We were ecstatic to be fathers of healthy boys who looked like tiny replicas of ourselves. About a year after he sent me those photos, he was gone. It's been almost ten years since their births, and our boys are quickly turning into young men. It seemed like everything we had done together was all over—no more lifting weights, no more nights working in a club filled with patrons. Even though our routines had changed, we never stopped being gym rats. We both still found time to stay in shape. The day that he died, he had just gone to the gym.

Anthony loved life and was always energetic. Having this innate gift made him a great father. The day of his death started no differently than any other day in his life. He woke up to the screams of his hungry twenty-one-month-old little boy and jumped out of bed to give his wife time to rest. Anthony once told me that seeing his son in the morning gave him a feeling of euphoria, like that of a child when the sun is shining through the window on Christmas morning. It's time to get up! He walked into his son's room and saw him standing with his hands on the crib's railing. Soon after Anthony took his boy out of the crib and cradled him in his arms, his wife, Cindy, walked into the room. She saw her baby boy Anthony Jr. (or as they called him, AJ) lying with his head on his daddy's broad shoulder with those large half-moon eyes looking at her. She took AJ from Anthony so he could get ready for work and then made breakfast for the family while Anthony showered. He came downstairs, ate, and then kissed his wife and child goodbye for what would be the last time.

After work, Cindy would run errands and then pick up AJ from daycare. Anthony would work all day and then go to the gym. This schedule worked well for them because they would arrive at home around the same time. Usually, Cindy would make it home first, but on this day, her errands took a little longer because she wanted to pick up a few ingredients for a special dinner. She went to the store, got AJ up from day care, and came home. Cindy pulled into the driveway to find that Anthony's car was parked in front of the house. She was relieved because bringing in groceries with a rambunctious little boy was difficult. She opened the door and came in with a few bags in one hand and AJ's hand in the other. She put down her bags on the island in the kitchen and called for Anthony. There was no answer. She assumed that he might have been upstairs either ready to take a shower or getting dressed after showering.

She smiled at AJ and said, "Let's run up the stairs to get Daddy."

AJ smiled, and Cindy ran up to the bedroom with AJ in her arms. The door was cracked. Cindy put AJ down on his wobbly but mobile legs. Pushing the door wide open, he awkwardly ran into the room. AJ stopped in midstride and collapsed on to his backside with his feet out in front of him.

There was Anthony, lying on the bed, fresh out of the shower and dressed to relax for the night. The soles of his feet were facing AJ and Cindy at the foot of the bed.

AJ said, "Mommy, Daddy sleeping."

Anthony's toes were pointing upward toward the slowly spinning ceiling fan above him. She assumed he was sleeping, too. Cindy figured she would wake him from his catnap so he could watch AJ while she grabbed the rest of the groceries. As she moved closer, she saw his face and realized his eyes were wide open. She grabbed him and shook him vigorously. Anthony did not respond. She started to think the worst, checked his vitals, and realized he might be gone. Cindy held in her pain so as not to startle AJ and closed Anthony's eyes before calling 911. She knew it was probably too late, but she had to try. AJ and Cindy lay by Anthony's side, waiting for the wailing of sirens to indicate emergency vehicles were close. She lay next to Anthony and sobbed with her salty tears running down her face. AJ was curled up against Cindy's side and was silent. It was obvious that AJ felt the presence of something ominous. Soon the ambulance would arrive and confirm that Anthony had expired. She could not find the words to explain to AJ what had happened to his beloved father.

Anthony had a massive heart attack that day after coming home from the gym. I could not imagine the lasting effects associated with seeing your husband lying on the bed never to rise again. I will never forget the day that I heard he was gone or the story that was passed down to me of what happened to him. From that day on, I promised to do a better job of keeping in contact with my friends and all the people I loved. It freaked me out to think of how that could have been me on that bed. I work out all the time. My wife and child could have walked into our bedroom and found me like that. Hearing about Anthony changed the way I thought about life. The ideas that come with being young and feeling invincible were replaced with thoughts of how best to provide for my family if I were no longer here. I developed a newfound understanding that anyone can be here one day and gone the next.

Anthony's death brought back the memories of the time before I had a wife and a son, the era before my colleagues addressed me with the title of doctor. This was the time in my life when I went from a young, independent college graduate to a man. It got me reminiscing about the past and various people I would never have encountered if it hadn't been for the club. The club influenced my life and helped me understand the world to a greater extent. These thoughts propelled me to write this memoir.

## CHAPTER 2
# MIDDLE MANAGEMENT

I was exposed to the nightlife in 2000, when I was twenty-one. My matriculation at a local university in the capital of Delaware was quickly coming to an end when I met a mountain of a man who would introduce me to the world of bouncing. He weighed every bit of three hundred pounds, and at six feet three inches tall, he was an imposing figure. He would become the person I should thank for introducing me to the supplemental income that would pay for my first apartment, a master's degree in curriculum and instruction, and my doctorate in education. His name was Horse. Aside from referring to his size, the name came because he grew up on a farm that raised horses.

Horse and I first crossed paths on a fall day during my daily workout at the local gym. I had a bizarre feeling that day because I could feel more eyes than usual paying close attention to my intense lifting regimen. I found out a couple of years later from a guy we hired at the club that there was a rumor at the gym about me. The word around the campfire was that the under-six-foot diesel-black guy with the intense workout was on steroids. I am sure this came from one of the many part-time exercise enthusiasts who watched me lift.

My workout consisted of starting on the bench with 135 pounds, which I would lift twenty times. Then I would add two large plates, bringing the weight to 225 pounds and lift that ten times. I would add another large plate to each side of the bar, bringing the weight to 315 pounds. I bench-pressed this weight about five to eight times. On a good day, I would continue adding more weight to about 325 pounds and complete three reps before I reduced the weight and repeated the sequence in reverse order until I completed a grueling, culminating set of 135 pounds lifted twenty times. Believe it or not, I still had enough in the tank to lift 120-pound dumbbells for multiple sets. The funny thing is that most spectators never noticed that I ran a few miles to warm up before I lifted anything. I was still in good shape after I stopped playing football in college in 1997 and disappointed my father greatly with that decision. My parents had dreamed of me attending their alma mater, and my father loved the idea of me playing football where he had.

The day I met Horse, he watched very closely as I added more and more weight while lifting on the flat bench. I typically lifted alone and at varying times of night because the gym was open twenty-four hours. I was a loner, which meant I needed to ask strangers to spot me on heavy lifts. This day, I felt extremely good and took a shot at four hundred pounds. I got a couple of guys to watch me lift in case it was too much for me, but it was not the first time I had lifted this, and I knew I would be fine. They spotted me on opposite sides of the bar and watched in amazement while this relatively normal-sized individual took this dense amount of weight and brought it not once but twice down to his chest before extending his arms to put the bar back on the rack. I sat up and took a deep breath with my head looking down at the floor. The sweat rolled across my forehead and slowly dripped down. I wiped my brow and inhaled deeply.

In the corner of my eye, I saw this figure walking over to me. I turned toward him, and he said, "Impressive!"

I said, "Thanks."

That was my first encounter with Horse. His next statement puzzled me. "Do you want a job?"

I smirked and squinted my eyes so tight that my eyebrows moved close together into the shape of a *V*. Horse stepped back, rubbing the thinning blond hairs on the top of his head with massive fingers that were as thick as bratwursts. He explained that he was the head of security at a local restaurant and bar. He said, "We need a new guy at the bar to work the door."

I started to remove the additional weight from the bench, and he assisted me while attempting to sell me on the limited job duties affiliated with this opportunity. Horse said, "All you do is check IDs and sit at the door to make sure nothing happens." He kept adding to the list of incentives by telling me about the free meal with every shift and the pay of fifty bucks under the table each night.

Of course, I asked about how many people I would be working with, and he said, "You will be working alone." I was leery about pursuing the job, but I was in college, making a few dollars on campus as an academic coach, and this was cash money. Also, I would work only one night a week.

I asked, "Am I big enough to do this kind of job?"

He paused, standing straight up with his barrel of a chest sticking out, and looked me right in the eyes. He said, "Believe me, with your build, nobody is going to test you, buddy."

I took his number and said, "I'll think about it."

For days, I contemplated if I should take the job. I was living on campus for free because I was one of the students who worked at the university's apartment complex.

I needed to make more money to ensure my independence from my parents while I finished college. I really wanted to prove to my father that I could take care of myself. He always told me, "You're not living here with me and your mother after high school." Having a job that did not interfere with school could be another step in the direction of independence. After thinking it over, I called Horse and accepted his offer. We met at the bar in a small shopping mall with a pizza place, a bank, and a liquor store.

The place was a combination bar and restaurant with a bar to the left and a dining area to the right. It was a watering hole for blue-collar guys to stop in for a beer and local families to grab a bite to eat.

On my first night, Horse met me at the restaurant early enough to explain the ropes and for me to eat my free meal. Horse introduced me to the waitstaff and the bartenders. Everyone seemed nice. Horse pointed out the owner in the distance. His receding hairline kept what few thinning dark curls he had covering the budding bald spot on top of his head. He wore an athletic suit. His shirt was unbuttoned enough to see his dark, curly chest hairs strangling a small gold chain. The necklace was glistening beneath what looked to be at least two or three extra chins with stubble on them. He was so large that when he walked across the restaurant, he would run out of breath and pause, gasping for oxygen in the smoke-filled room. This was a couple of years before Delaware's governor signed the bill that prohibited smoking in establishments like this one.

I finished eating, and Horse took me to meet the owner, whom I privately called the Fat Man. This nickname was a result of hearing and witnessing his disrespectful behavior. I respect all I meet, and it is their job to keep that respect. He obviously lost mine quickly. The Fat Man glanced in our direction and looked at me for a second to acknowledge my presence but fast enough to avoid a formal introduction with a handshake.

During this first night, everything was fine until the Fat Man walked by, and I told him, "I appreciate you giving me the opportunity to work in your establishment."

The Fat Man looked at me and said, "Don't thank me. I didn't hire you." At this point, I was not sure if he was having a bad night or if the Fat Man was not fond of African Americans. I tried to avoid jumping to a conclusion based on race and convinced myself I was not meeting his expectations.

Soon after that interaction, my night got worse.

I made the common rookie mistakes. I let in a twenty-year-old with a fake ID, and the Fat Man wouldn't even look at me afterward. He was perturbed, and it became abundantly clear he did not want me there.

Then a bartender told me a couple of guys had had a few too many and needed to leave. I approached them, and Horse was near because there were two guys and only me.

They had paid their tab, and I nicely asked them to leave. One gentleman told his friend, "Let's just go." The drunker of the two wore a red polo with a stain on the collar; he stood up and looked down at me. He looked into my eyes deeply for a few seconds, but it seemed like minutes. I smiled and said, "Have a nice evening, sir," then pointed to the door.

Red Polo said, "Make me leave. My ass is staying right here."

Horse moved behind me, and Red Polo's friend tugged on his arm. They walked to the door and slammed it shut as they stormed toward the parking lot. It was over.

Horse told me I did a good job but if they needed to be tossed out, "Make sure you open the door with their head."

The night was about over, and the patrons were about to leave. All I had left to do was walk out the waitresses with their earnings for the night. The cook came out and told me that I had done well. Then he said, "Here is some dessert for you to take home. It's time for me to go next door and get myself a Two Eleven Steel Reserve."

I smiled and nodded. He came back a few minutes later with his malt liquor in a brown paper bag. He put it in the refrigerator until he finished cleaning the kitchen. He had a unique ritual. At the end of every night, he would take his 211 and drink it on his walk home. By the time, he made it home, the can was empty. What he did next always fascinated me. He would take ten dollars out of his pocket to give to the local dealer at his apartment building for one crack rock. He'd toss the empty beer can into the garbage and adjourn upstairs to smoke his rock and pass out for the night. He was the first functioning crack addict I had ever seen.

As time passed, I learned a lot about the Fat Man and about myself. The biggest thing I learned was that the Fat Man had fired a guy named T, who was the bouncer I'd replaced. I learned this from a former bartender named Layla, who had returned from a college on the West Coast. She'd decided to finish school back east and get her job back at the bar.

Layla said, "They called him T because he wanted to be like his idol, Mr. T," the chain-wearing tough guy from the 1980s television show *The A-Team*. It was obvious that he was stuck in the eighties. She was renting him a basement apartment in a house that her family owned.

Layla told me why T had been fired. It was interesting. Like most bar tales, it starts with a young girl, working as a waitress and trying to become something greater. Her name was Megan, and she had big, red, curly hair. Layla explained that the repugnant Fat Man essentially used a quid pro quo approach to woo her. On many occasions, the Fat Man offered her a raise for spending time with him. Megan declined out of sheer revulsion. Once, he even cornered her in the kitchen and kissed her during cleanup at the end of her shift. He grabbed the back of her head and pulled her face to his. His several chins smothered her, poking her with protruding stubble. He shoved his tongue into her mouth, and she kissed him back for a second out of fear. Then, with disgust, she quickly pushed him away. He laughed as she stood there in shock.

Layla told me the Fat Man was married but had tried to have sex with every young girl at the bar. He was not shy. Without hesitation, he tested the waters, taking his greasy hand and clutching any firm backside within reach while making sexually explicit comments. I despised this type of disrespectful behavior.

One night, T was waiting to walk out the waitresses, and Megan was procrastinating so that she would be last and leave with T without anyone noticing. They walked out to the parking lot and got into her car. Not many people paid enough attention to notice that Megan and T were growing close, but Layla had her suspicions.

The Fat Man ran out to his car to get a cigarette and saw her car in the parking lot with the windows fogged up. He walked over to see if she was OK, since she should have left about ten minutes before. The Fat Man saw T in the passenger's seat with it reclined as far back as possible. He looked closer to find that Megan's curls were bobbing up and down violently in T's lap.

The Fat Man banged on the car, telling them to leave. As the sound echoed into the car from the large, thunderous clap his palm made, Megan raised her head up from T's lap, embarrassed and scared, wiping saliva that had run down her chin from her award-winning act of fellatio.

Megan was like a deer in headlights, her eyes open like two full moons. She glared at the Fat Man between the strands of crimped red hair dangling in her face. T quickly sat up and covered up. The Fat man fired T on the spot for being able to obtain the unobtainable.

Megan drove off recklessly, hitting the side of the curb on the way out of the parking lot. The Fat Man stormed back into the bar, telling everyone what he'd just witnessed. He was so angry that he had kissed the girl who was sucking his bouncer's unit!

Layla also told me of the advances that the Fat Man made toward her. She was a victim of his frequent, abrasive passes. She was an extremely smart woman and had an amazing body with curves like a road in the valley. Like me, she was in her early twenties and in college. She had braces that made her look like a mature schoolgirl. I did not realize that she would turn into a friend for life.

As fate would have it, I met T once while I worked at the restaurant and another time while working in a different establishment. This man was about six foot five with the longest fingernails I'd ever seen on a man. His nails had dirt that was as dark as coal underneath. The joke he told me was that if he ever got into a jam, he could claw his way out. I assumed that would probably leave someone with a disgusting infection. His face looked damaged by the hard living associated with a life of labor-intensive day jobs followed by long, sleepless nights in bars. The wrinkles under his eyes were deep, leaving profound, dark half circles. He was in his forties, telling me how he was retired but still working for this nightspot around the corner that a group of Masons owned.

This place had parties about once a month. Ironically, one of the Masons named Skip came into the bar the same night I met T. He was a slender man with a thin mustache that looked like it was dyed with black shoe polish. We talked, and he liked me enough to give me his card. He said, "Call me." He told me he needed some new guys like me at his establishment. I had no idea I would need that card sooner than later.

I unexpectedly quit my job at the restaurant due to an inevitable, unforeseeable event a few weeks after meeting

Layla, Skip, and the legendary T. I had no idea that I would be forced into a short retirement, but I had at least caught on to how the game was played. I could spot a fake ID a mile away. If I wasn't sure if an ID was fake, I asked a question like, "Do I know you? You live at Fifty-Two Whatever Lane, right?" Basically, I would look at the ID and learn the address but give the wrong house number to see if the patron noticed. I had started using numerous tricks like this to get a better feel for who might be lying.

My last night was a special one. The bar was packed. Every patron's hands were covered in a generic, burgundy wing sauce. Even though the cook was amazing, he couldn't help that the Fat Man preferred a basic, tasteless hot-wing sauce. People were in every seat. It was late, and around this time, minors would try to sit with older friends way in the back of the restaurant and share alcoholic beverages. This night, a thick, gray film of cigarette smoke filled the place.

A frail, older gentleman timidly walked to the front entrance of the restaurant from outside. He looked from left to right, as if he were fearful of something happening if he came in to have a drink. I said, "Hey, what's up?"

He looked at me for a second. He contemplated responding. He fearfully said, "My name is Raymond. Is it all right for me to come in?"

I said, "Raymond, I will take care of you, and I promise nothing will happen if you come in for a beer."

He smiled with a mouth full of teeth with black spots and came into the establishment.

Just then, I heard commotion from the back of the restaurant. I had the foresight to know what was probably going to take place and walked to the back. I watched a group of couples closely as I sauntered to the rear. I simply told them it was important for those individuals twenty-one and older to keep their drinks in front of them. I said it in a way that sounded like I was asking them to do me a favor but was firm enough to imply that inability to cooperate could result in a change in my demeanor. I also liked to be courteous so if it became physical, no one could say I was belligerent. I also needed them to know that I was watching them because they had gotten loud and rowdy. The most offensive member of the group patted me on the back and said he would keep everyone cool. That was at 11:30 p.m.

An hour later, the very person who said he would keep everything cool was swinging for the fences. All you could see were fists going up and down from across the room. People quickly moved to avoid getting hit by these wild punches. I ran back to the altercation. Two guys rolled on the floor. I grabbed the one on top and pulled him off. I pushed him back and told him to stay back. As I turned around, this hand came straight toward my face. The drunken kid I had spoken with from the group prior had hit me with all his might. I didn't flinch. I stared at him so deeply I could have seen his soul rise out of his body. He was petrified. He stood in front of me with his hands up, palms forward, as if I were robbing him. He was praying I would not return the favor. I mean, what other option did he have? He hit me with his best shot and realized it didn't bother me. His friends stood up and backed away from the table.

I simply said, "Pick up your shit, pay your tab, and get the fuck out before I respond in a way that leaves one of us paralyzed from the waist down."

They grabbed everything quickly like the place was on fire, asking me repeatedly if we were cool. I told them, "It's not cool, but it's OK." I trailed them to the door.

As I turned around, Raymond immediately came to see if I was all right. I started to realize that he might be a little mentally challenged but nothing debilitating. I assured him I was fine, and he exhaled with a sigh of relief.

It was the end of the night. The entire staff and several patrons by this time had seen me drag out and choke out a few individuals who were hard of hearing when given direction. While the staff was cleaning up and counting money and the cook was about to walk home with his frosty beverage, I sat waiting for the waitresses so I could walk them out. The Fat Man and his friend had started talking about a regular black patron. I heard the Fat Man call him an "arrogant middle-management nigger."

I stood up to address the situation, but Layla came over after seeing my expression. She said, "Honey, we're OK tonight," and gave me my money to go home. These moments for young African Americans like myself are never forgotten, and in this case, never forgiven, either. Without Layla getting me out of the bar that night, I would have sat there, contemplating how to retaliate on behalf of all those who had been impacted by ignorant individuals like this. I still wonder at times what I might have done.

I found out years later after talking to Layla that the Fat Man had Mafia ties. That was how he got the money to buy the bar and restaurant. He felt entitled and invincible because of his wife's Italian mob family. I left, never to work there again.

I did stop by the bar after it was under new management but only a couple of times. I regret walking out that night without saying anything or hitting that fat bastard across the head with one of the barstools. I knew as a college student who would embark on a career in education, that a felony would put my degree to waste.

# CHAPTER 3
# THE MASONS

My funds were limited after quitting my part-time job at the bar. I was still working on campus as an academic coach, and I was fortunate to acquire another job working for the university police force as a student cadet. These jobs provided very little capital because the hours I worked were limited to maybe fifteen a week. This would not suffice for my goal of financial independence from my parents. In addition, I needed to save money for a class in the summer. Without the regular income from another bouncing job, I would need to ask my parents for the money or max out a credit card. To make things worse, after that semester, I would not be able to keep my free apartment because only students with a full year of classes could work and stay rent-free. I was down to my last semester. I needed money to make my dream a reality. I would be completing my minor and, with several weeks of student teaching, finishing my degree requirements for my bachelor's in the fall. It was difficult going to school out of state with my family miles away in New Jersey, greatly reducing the options I had for support.

I was desperate to make something happen, so I called Skip. There was no answer. I left a message. I called a couple times a week for almost a month. I left only the one message but kept calling and calling and calling. I was on the verge of accepting my fate when I decided to call one last time. If there were no answer, I would call my folks or use the dreaded credit card for summer school. I also would need a plan for how to stay on campus for my last semester. Regardless, I would do my best not to ask my folks for money. I wanted to prove to myself and my father that I could take care of myself.

I made the call, and Skip finally answered. He said that he had an event coming up and that I could work it. He offered me sixty-five dollars for the night. I had been making fifty dollars a night at the restaurant, so even for only a night, this would be a raise. This could be a great opportunity. The only problem was that the Masons had events just once or twice a month. That wasn't enough supplemental income, even with my campus jobs.

I told a college friend who was a local to the area about my doing security at the Masons' after-hours spot, and he said, "Are you sure you want to work at that place?"

His question puzzled me, and I frowned.

He said, "You must know the story."

I replied, "What story?" I sat down to listen to this legendary tale.

About two years earlier, the Masons had a huge party. The core group of partygoers were Masons and established people over thirty-five years old. However, their events were known to bring out the local criminal element as well. There was a unique mixture of Masons, an abundance of older, attractive women referred to as cougars, and of course, the nefarious criminal element, which made this night unique. Whenever attractive women of any age are involved, things can quickly crescendo into chaos. The ballroom was filled with men in suits who represented every Crayola color. Almost all of them had large, magnificent rings resembling the accessories worn by Super Bowl champions. Like most nights, there was music, alcohol, and the courting that occurs between the sexes.

It's inevitable that these good vibes will change. Some say that the start of the tension occurred because a divorced couple who came separately got into a verbal squabble because the woman showed up with her new love interest. Her ex calmed down, but this was the start of the atmosphere going from jubilant to ominous. The crowd at the beginning of the night might have been thirty-five and older, but as the night progressed, it became closer to twenty-one.

My buddy explained that as the night advanced, the attire went quickly from suits and ties to white T-shirts and jeans. The younger element was rude and uncouth. The elder statesmen looked at everyone who was not a Mason as someone let in just to contribute to the funds taken at the door.

The night was about to end, and many individuals started to make their way to the exits. All the Masons and their significant others stayed inside, while all of those young, rebellious, ill-mannered locals moved the party into the parking lot. They played loud music, yelled, and cursed over the thunderous bass lines coming from the subwoofers in one of the cars. This was a recurring issue for the local neighborhoods. The noise would resonate from the parking lot to their homes.

Like clockwork, two men began arguing in the parking lot. Then the associates of the two men started to fight. This led to several individuals engaging in physical altercations. Fights began popping up all over the parking lot like firecrackers going off. Then Skip locked the doors to the building and called the police. The neighbors, however, had already beat him to it.

As the fighting continued, one group started to take the momentum of the battle by grabbing one individual and beating him unmercifully. Others began to drive off as fast as possible at high speeds around bodies embraced in a waltz resembling a real version of *West Side Story*. You could hear screams from females, the screeching from car tires, and the commotion that comes from crowds verbalizing what they are witnessing.

Sirens sounded in the distance, and the participants of an all-out brawl started to disperse. One group got into a sedan. All four doors were open, and three men jumped into the car. A fourth man was still fighting as his associates told him to stop and get in the car. He was straddling someone, landing punch after punch. He got up with blood dripping from his knuckles and moved toward the car, grabbing the left leg of the beaten man and sitting in the car.

The driver yelled, "Let him go!"

The car started to speed off, and the door slammed violently, like it was caught in the wind, on the leg of the beaten man. The door continued to open and close on his leg as they swerved around speed bumps and other cars in the parking lot. The car dragged the man, his head bouncing off the ground, hitting every bump beneath him and drifting him into unconsciousness.

The flashing lights were visible now, and the guy in the car let go of the man's leg, leaving his body between the dotted yellow lines in the middle of the street. He was just a bloody vessel lying on the ground. The police saw him and immediately got him to the hospital to be declared DOA.

That story gave me the understanding that my role at this nightspot was to keep out the undesirables. There probably would not be issues inside. I assumed my job would be to take money at the door and turn away unscrupulous individuals who would want to enter. I took that story to heart and learned a good lesson that made me wiser when it came to picking security jobs in the future. I would always know the type of patrons the establishment catered to and if it was worth the risk.

I showed up at eight o'clock sharp to meet Skip outside. Skip had on a blue Stacy Adams suit with what looked to be thousand-dollar Mauri gator shoes. I mean, he was sharp! We went into the building through the glass double doors in front. We sat in his office, and he said that I would be taking the money at the front door. It was exactly what I was expecting.

He said, "Do not let anyone in who is under twenty-five."

After the story I'd heard, I knew why. There was a knock on the office door. Skip opened it.

Standing there in a tattered blue dress shirt was the statuesque T. He came in and shook my hand with a firm handshake. He remembered me from the restaurant. Even in his nice attire, he still had dirt under his fingernails. We would be working together that night.

Soon after, Skip introduced me to every ring-wearing associate in the place. They were dressed like deacons from a church or pimps from the streets, depending on your vantage point. Regardless of their apparel, they were all cooler than the draft that hits you when you first get out of the shower. The tour Skip gave me also introduced me to the women frying fish and chicken in the kitchen. The aroma of the food filled the room like the smoke from the fryer. A small-framed opening used to take orders was on the side of the kitchen facing a large dance floor.

I went to my post and checked IDs and let everyone who was wearing a ring in for free. One individual walked by without speaking. I said, "Excuse me, sir. We have a ten-dollar cover this evening."

He stopped walking and turned his head, looking at me over his right shoulder from the corner of his eyes. He slowly took a few steps toward me with a smirk on his face. He put one hand on my shoulder. The other was balled into a fist. He raised that fist up to my face, almost blinding me with his polished ring. Then he said, "This ring is all I need to enter, youngblood."

I told him I hadn't seen the ring. He just maintained his arrogant attitude and walked away smirking, signifying that he was superior to me. I was not happy about being belittled. Looking back on it, though, I think it's kind of funny. Ring or no ring, no man can see what the future holds. I wonder what hand life has dealt him since our encounter. I, for one, have become relatively successful as time passed.

I spent the night getting to know some real cool gentlemen while I worked the door. T spent the night mingling with a handful of desperate, big-assed, needy cougars. I mean, these women were mature, with bodies held together by all kinds of elastic under their dresses. I was sure whomever he took home was going to slip out of her clothes and fall into a pile of goo on the floor. The night soon ended, and I got paid. Unfortunately, while we were getting all the ringless guests out and sorting out what mistresses could stay inside, a bang echoed from the front of the building. It came from the glass door up front. Someone had come by and cracked the door with a brick. Skip was furious. He was yelling about how one of us should have been at the front door while the other stayed inside, coaxing the patrons to leave. I remember thinking that if more than one of us were working, this would not have happened. T had spent his night trying to penetrate the female genitalia of someone's grandmother while I had done all of the work.

Either way, I got paid and realized that I would never work there again. I decided that I might need to find a steady job. My college friend Abdulla worked at a local club. He told me that I should stop by and talk to the owners during the daytime. He said I could use him as a reference. Abdulla and I had met playing football in college. He was a linebacker, and I was a safety. Who would have known that this acquaintance would lead me to the most memorable experience of my life?

## CHAPTER 4
# THE CLUB

I took Abdulla's advice and stopped by the club every day to talk with one of the owners about a job. My plan was simple. On my heavy-lifting gym days, I wore a tight shirt, got as pumped as possible, and then stopped by the club with the hope of making a good first impression. Several weeks went by before I caught one of the owners. The day I met one, I remember thinking, *Finally, I have a chance.*

The owner's name was Remus. I gave him my number after some small talk. He was a skinny guy with glasses. By far the biggest Patriots fan I have ever met. Remus had no kids and was single. I still can picture him in his old, white skater sneakers with khaki shorts and a faded polo.

I waited day after day to receive a call, but it never came. I continued my workouts followed by a club drive-by. The club was open only Thursday, Friday, and Saturday nights. I was contemplating just stopping in during one of their open nights when the unexpected happened. I visited as usual after my workout, and Remus told me to come in Thursday at

9:00 p.m. It was perfect! I knew if this did not work, I would need to figure out how else to pay for summer school and afford my apartment in the fall.

Thursday night came quickly. Even though I was in college, this club would provide me the best education about the people in the world. I showed up to work on that first night and parked my car right in front. I realized very quickly that this place was not like the music videos on television. The club shared a building that housed a hotel. Upon realizing that, I parked my car in front of the hotel. I saw the thrifty early patrons congregating in the parking lot. They knew that if they came early enough, there would be no cover. I got out of my white 1989 Dodge Shadow and proceeded to walk through the small crowd in front.

As I walked up to the door, I saw a figure who looked to be around four hundred pounds. The shadow that he cast was like a large sequoia or skyscraper. He stopped me and asked for my ID with his large palm facing up and his arm extended. Then I saw Remus walking toward the front door. He saw me and waved me in before I could respond to the massive man's request. Remus introduced me to the imposing figure and explained that he was the head doorman. His name was Rushmore or Rush for short. The name came from his build being reminiscent of the mountain covered with the faces of dead presidents.

Remus told me to wait at the doorway while he went into the office, which was up front on the left as we entered. He said he needed to make a quick phone call. I stood at the front door and looked around, watching the flashing lights from inside flicker in hues of red, yellow, and blue. I perused the layout.

The front door had a small camera next to it used to record the IDs checked. When the music was loud, the camera would vibrate a little and would go in and out of focus. At the time, I did not comprehend the significance of the camera. Later, I would find out the need for this.

I turned to the right and saw the cash register. There was a slight ramp from the door to the vast opening to the club. At the top of the ramp, everything inside looked black: black tables, black chairs, and of course, black walls. The bar was to the left and wrapped around the entire left side of the wall. The club had pub-style circular tables with barstools in front. Behind them were the dance floor and the DJ booth. I put my hand on the railing and felt the vibrations from the bass in the music. The lights glimmered and turned like an airport landing strip. The vast space seemed unoccupied except for a few bartenders and the barback aiding them in their last-minute preparation.

The barback was running back and forth with buckets of ice, cases of beer, and bottles of liquor. He was a skinny guy with lots of energy. His name was Simon. His father was white, and his mother was Korean. Simon was a black belt in jeet kune do and wanted nothing more than to be one of the bouncers.

One night, an attractive African American woman arose from the masses like a phoenix. I told Simon, "You should talk to her, ask her out."

Simon replied, "No offense. I mean, she is hot, but I can't date outside of my race."

My face frowned as if the most profound odor had entered the room. I said with a smile filled with confusion, "But you're white and Korean."

## The Other Side of the Velvet Rope

He said he had been raised to think that way. I just stood my ground and said nothing more. I never understood the logic behind that kind of thinking.

Soon, Remus came out of the office and handed me a canary-colored shirt with the word *staff* in all-black capital letters on the back. I put on the shirt, and we began to walk. He explained to me how my job was to walk around and pick up empty glasses during the night. I could see several other doormen walking up the ramp, each one looking larger than the last. I felt like a bulldog among mastiffs, rottweilers, and Great Danes.

Remus quickly introduced me to all the people there, but they seemed uninterested in greeting me. We continued to walk around the bar, and I met the bartenders. We walked across the dance floor, and I met Jason Romulus, the other owner. His wife helped by bartending at times. He was a tall, slender man holding a light beer. He had a low-cut beard that could not hide the look of inquisitiveness on his face. It was obvious he was curious as to why his partner had hired this little guy. He had the same body language that the other staff did. I did not understand why they were so distant until years later.

The staff and a few regular patrons started to come into the club. I talked briefly with one bouncer named Burt. He was a truck driver who was real cool. He was a little older with a bald spot on the top of his head that would reflect the club's flashing lights. We stayed in touch, even though soon after I arrived at the club, he left. After Burt and I talked for a few, he walked off, and I ran into a regular named Jimmy. He was always telling jokes and picking on the staff. He was just one of the guys. Jimmy was a frail little black guy with a unique passion: he loved obese white women. We joked with him about that all the time. He would say with a devilish grin, "So what if I like fat white girls? They treat me good, and that's all that matters."

He would always break down and tell us how he just loved every type of woman. Tall, fat, ugly—he didn't care as long as she was female.

Jimmy spent his club nights drinking and challenging us with verbal banter. My first night, he just looked at me with a smile and said, "You won't make it through the night."

I smiled, but deep down, I hoped he was not right.

Then I saw Abdulla pull up. He drove a nice, clean, almost-new red Mustang. He looked different than he did at school. His shrunken yellow shirt made his six-foot, 240-pound frame look more imposing than anyone I had ever seen. He had his hair braided and wore a low-cut beard. He was quick to show me the ins and outs of working at this club. Abdulla knew a lot about this scene because he'd had experience in a few New York City clubs. He was a few years older than I was. He spoke to the other bouncers on his way over to me.

He said, "Finally, you made it." He was smiling from ear to ear.

He started telling me about the type of people who frequented the club. "Just like any other job, avoid taking your work home with you. These chicks in here are scandalous and nothing but trouble."

I nodded in agreement. At this point, it would be safe to say that class was in session, and I was about to learn all about a unique world.

Abdulla pointed to a group of guys by the bar. These men did not exactly look like the entourage of anyone famous. He explained that they always came in early, as if they had no other place to go. I recognized some of them. They were the same guys who had been in the parking lot when I first arrived. There clothes looked tattered, and a few of them looked disheveled.

Abdulla singled one of them out and started to smile with a devilish grin. I said, "What?"

He said, "Can you see the guy with the yellowish teeth?"

"Yellow teeth?"

"Not yellow like gold. Yellow like butter." Then he pointed and said, "The one with the large T-shirt and tight jeans."

"Yeah."

Then Abdulla went on to tell me a crazy story. Basically, this individual was the leader of this weird group. One night, not too long ago, this leader of local misfits had met a misfit-ette, and they had begun to talk. He felt like the man. He was in the club, talking to this woman, whom Abdulla described as having King Kong's body and Medusa's face. They talked all night. At the end of the night, they were in the parking lot, hugged up and kissing. I wondered what kind of woman would swap spit with a man with yellow teeth. I couldn't imagine how repulsive his breath must have been. A patron who worked at a dentist's office once told me that he had more bacteria in his mouth than a community water fountain. The patron referred to his saliva as being acidic. That thought was nauseating. But I digress.

Then Abdulla's story took a quick turn. Not only was this dude trying to seal the deal with this dreadful-looking woman, but he had told the wife no one knew he had that he might need a ride home from the club. Of course, once she showed up, she found him draped all over another woman in the parking lot. He had his hands on her gelatinous backside, pulling her close to him. His wife could see them kissing and gazing into each other's eyes. All of this occurred right under the glow of a parking lot light post. The lovebirds had no idea that a woman scorned was about to interrupt them. She parked the car off to the side a few feet behind him in front of the club.

Abdulla said, "His wife was, like, three hundred pounds." She opened the car door, and the car rose about six inches. She got out, relieving the pressure on the strained, squeaky shocks of this dilapidated, blue, rusty vehicle.

She ran over to him, and he tried to play it cool and talk to her like he was in charge. He raised his voice, talking about how he could do what he wanted and she needed to respect his role as the man. His wife did not pause nor did she reply to his snide comments. She simply tilted her head to the left and took out one earring and then another. He continued to rant. His potential fling stepped to the side to avoid any confrontation and joined the crowd of voyeurs beginning to congregate around this spectacle.

He went on, saying things like, "Listen here, bitch! I can do whatever I damn well please." He started to feel superior as the onlookers oohed and aahed at his statements. He walked toward her with his index finger waving from left to right in her face. The scowl on his face was reminiscent of an angry parent disciplining a child.

Once he got close enough, she hit him in the mouth with a right and then a left. The security staff came outside and were entertained to the point of not interfering. She knocked him down and was on top of him, hitting him repeatedly. Then she got up and went to the car as he rolled over, spitting blood from his hemorrhaging lip.

Once at the car, she opened the door, leaned in, and pulled out his radio. The radio had two large speakers and a cassette-tape deck in the middle like the boom boxes of the late eighties. It was his prized possession from his youth, and he still used it almost daily. He had no car, but when he walked, he had his radio. She tossed it at his feet while he sat on the ground, angrily trying to conjure up a way to regain the masculine form he had displayed only minutes prior.

She said, "Take all your shit and agitate the gravel!" She went back into the car to toss out more of his belongings.

Just then, he jumped up off the ground, fueled by embarrassment, and grabbed the radio with his left hand. She was startled and hit him a few more times as he started to back up and raise his hands. He used the radio to cover up and avoid any more damage. Then out of fear, he hit her over the head with the radio. *Boom!* She hit the pavement, causing the Earth's plates to shift slightly, making the ground move beneath the spectators.

He stood there, standing over her with the radio in pieces. His eyes and mouth were wide open. He had surprised himself more than he had the crowd. She was unfazed and proceeded to get up to kill him. You could see the fire in her eyes. He saw that and ran like a rabbit that had been startled in the woods. He sprinted away, knowing she was too obese to follow and that his embarrassment would take on new heights if she got her hands on him again.

I guess he did not realize the humiliation associated with running. The crowd laughed out loud at this crazy episode. A few spectators came to her assistance while she cursed him under her breath, but she was fine—no physical damage, just emotional. I pondered the level of dysfunction that was associated with a portion of the club goers at this venue. This was not how civilized individuals conducted themselves.

After hearing the story, I remember asking Abdulla if they were still together. He said, "Yup."

"Why is she still with him?" I asked. "How, after all of that, could he still come out to the club?"

He said, "That's how things work in this environment. Some of these people live a life with very little, and it makes them hold on to whatever they have, no matter what happens. Understand things that seem of no value to us are, for some, all they have."

I was amazed. His story explained to me something about human nature I would never forget. People can be content with what they already know just because going into the unknown is too scary.

By now, the club had started to fill up, and my night of picking up glasses had commenced. I walked in circles, getting glasses and realizing that only the senior staff had posts to stand at for the duration of the shift. I saw Remus at the front door, controlling the entry of the clientele. Some came in for free, but most of them paid the cover. Romulus stayed in the DJ booth, making sure that the music selection did not incite a riot.

The crowd was full of everything from drug dealers and ex-cons to local college kids and random curious strangers who walked in for a change of atmosphere. Most of the women dressed like video vixens and prostitutes, wearing tight-fitting black dresses with stiletto heels. They were not flawless beauties like on TV. Many of them were hard on the eyes in the club's darkness and even worse when the lights were on.

The night moved quickly. Soon the night ended, and the lights came on. We coaxed the crowd to finish their drinks and get to their vehicles to leave. Out of nowhere from the murmur of conversation came a female shriek. Then the word *bitch* bellowed from the bar area. Two women started fighting. All eyes were fixated on this altercation.

I couldn't see over the crowd from my vantage point. I moved in that direction, splitting the audience enough to make my way to the scene. All I could see was one of our massive bouncers with his arms around a woman's waist, carrying her over his shoulder. She was kicking and swinging her hands while being rushed to the front door. The other woman was in a choke hold with one large, vascular arm wrapped around her neck from behind. He would squeeze tighter and tighter like a boa constrictor subduing its prey every time she tried to move. He was whispering in her ear, asking her, "Are you done yet?" It was crazy seeing him whisper to her ever so softly while her eyes bulged from the pressure. It was over as fast as it had started.

We finished getting the remaining individuals out of the club with a sense of urgency. Every night ended with us walking through the parking lot to persuade the crowd to disperse without incident. The club had a contract to pay local police officers time and a half to ensure safe nights. They mostly watched us yell and move the crowd while they got paid. Altercations in the parking lot ruined many great nights.

Once the parking lot was clear, we would start to clean up the club. I was cleaning out front in the parking lot with Abdulla. We swept and picked up discarded debris. We talked about how my first night went, and I explained my discontent at being a glass runner for the bar. He told me all that would change in due time. He explained that there were three types of yellow shirts: the guys who pick up glasses, the ones who solve problems, and the guys whose only purpose is to fill out a shirt. There were a select few who could really lead and take care of business. Abdulla said, "When the shit hits the fan, they will see which one you are."

While we were sweeping up, we saw a couple over in the shadows of the parking lot talking. It was a guy and a skinny female companion.

Abdulla did not know the skinny companion by name. However, he did recognize her face. Abdulla started laughing again with his signature sinister smirk and mumbled, "He's got another one."

I was curious after his first story and asked, "Got another what?"

He took a deep breath and said, "Allah, give me strength." Then the story started. He told me that one night a stranger to the area saw this woman out at another watering hole and started talking to her. They danced and talked all night. He bought her drinks and her girlfriends drinks, too. They eventually got a hotel room."

I said, "Wait. That is a skinny, unkempt woman. Did he have any standards?"

Abdulla said, "Nope."

Once in the hotel room, she went straight to the bathroom. Moments later, he heard the toilet flush and the faucet running for a minute. The water stopped, the door opened, and there she was, standing in the shadows of the doorway. She turned off all the lights and slowly came over to him. She pushed him onto the bed. He lay on his back with his feet dangling over the edge of the bed. She got on top of him and straddled him. She began to kiss him on his neck and took off his shirt to kiss him on his chest. He tried to grab her, and she grabbed his hands and threw them above his head on the bed. She said, "Don't move; you're mine tonight." She got up and stripped down to nothing but a thong. Then she took off each of his shoes, pulled his pants down and his boxers, too. His soldier was standing at attention. She commenced to stimulate him orally. He tried to reach out to take off her delicates, and she shouted, "No!" She said she had just started her monthly.

He sat up, fuming, but before he could expound on his disappointment, she explained that she noticed it when she went to the bathroom to freshen up. She offered an alternative cavity for this evening's events. Then they had wild, freaky anal intercourse. It was assumed that sodomy was a turn-on for this guy.

Abdulla said, "I heard he even proposed to her during and afterward."

I started speculating about what the big deal was about some dude proposing to a random chick. I thought maybe she had gold underneath her dress.

He noticed the puzzled look on my face as if I were staring into a bright light. He said, "She tucks!"

"Who tucks what?" That's when I realized that the girl was a guy. He would come in the club and other local bars as a man and a woman at times, looking for his next unaware lover. Now, I understood that the skinny woman was really a skinny man! He spent many nights as a woman, looking for inebriated male partygoers who were desperate to find someone for coitus. He would typically lure them into the hotel next door. Once any moves were made to his nether regions, he would stop all physical action. Then he would play like he was embarrassed and say that he was menstruating.

This ambiguous figure was friends with the female bouncer who worked at the club. She was not working on my first night, but in due time, I would meet her. She did pat downs on the women at the door. She told Abdulla the story she'd heard from her cross-dressing, deceiving associate. She called herself a stud, meaning she was a gay female that played the role of the masculine partner in the relationship. For that reason, she had the nickname "Stud." Soon, she would tell some interesting stories of her own.

We finished cleaning, and before I parted, I asked Remus when I could work again. He said, "I'll see you next Thursday."

I went home fifty bucks richer, and I thought that this might be a perfect part-time job. I was not working alone, and even though the crowd was suspect, I thought it would be a good job that wouldn't interfere with school. I could afford summer school and my apartment if I got a bouncing shift every night the club was open. Most importantly, I learned a lot from Abdulla.

During our conversation at the end of that night he reiterated to me, "Never take your work home with you."

# CHAPTER 5
# UNDER TWENTY-ONE

After a couple of weeks of working at the club only one night a week, I established myself as more than a fetcher of empty glasses. I had not had the opportunity to throw anyone out yet, but I was getting respect for being on the scene to back up anyone who had a potentially violent situation.

Around this time, Remus asked me to work on Thursdays and Saturdays. These were the busiest nights. This place held a max of about five hundred people, and on those nights, the club averaged around four hundred fifty patrons. From certain angles, I could look over the crowd and see nothing more than a sea of heads bobbing up and down to the music, like waves in the ocean. The cigarette smoke from that many people in a box was irritating. One night I came back to my college apartment after work, and I was so tired I just tossed my shirt on the foot of my comforter. The next morning, the corner of my bed had absorbed the smoke from my shirt, giving off this putrid stench. I had to wash the shirt and the comforter a couple of times to get it out.

I was working and going to school, and between my campus jobs and the cash I earned under the table, life was good. Then Remus came to me with a way to make some extra money. He asked me and a select few if we could come in on Sunday night for an under-twenty-one event. The club had a few local high school kids who would promote these under-twenty-one nights at the club. They typically took place on holiday weekends when the kids were off on a Monday. This way the club would be open its regular nights and then make Sunday night a bonus payday. All the liquor would be locked away in the back storage area. One bartender would work to provide only soda for the kids to drink for a couple of dollars. They made good money on the door, charging these kids ten dollars just to enter. The door would make about $2,500, and their expenses with staff, the DJ, and the few bucks they gave the kids for promoting the night came to about $600.

The first under-twenty-one night I worked was one of the last times Remus and Romulus took a chance on making money with crazy, horny teens. Like all nights, it started slow, with the staff trickling in between 9:00 p.m. and 9:15 p.m. These nights picked up very quickly. This was the night that I got to know Anthony. He did not work every night, but he did work regularly. He was an IT guy who worked on computers during the day for a private company. On this night, I remembered us talking about football and old movies. We realized that we had some common interests.

The more innocent kids would always arrive early. At first, the atmosphere was reminiscent of a school dance:

young girls and boys awkwardly walking in small groups into this dark room full of thunderous sound and flashing lights. One of the girls was smitten with Abdulla. She was a full-figured redhead with eyes for him. I always remembered her by the freckles on her face and her large hips below her waist. She was about nineteen or twenty years old and assumed he might be interested in her if she pursued him. He stood at his usual spot on one of the corners of the dance floor. The redheaded vixen started to stand about a few feet from him with some friends, just staring and grinning at him. He glanced back and ignored her. Abdulla figured out that she was checking him out. It wasn't her fault for being attracted to him. He had women of all ages pursuing him. Abdulla was a lady's man. She just couldn't stop staring at him. She squinted at him as the lights flashed in her freckled face. Her top row of teeth was clamped down on her bottom lip. He looked back again after feeling her ogling him. He was getting frustrated. The giggles from the young girl and a couple of her associates irritated Abdulla even more. They started to move closer by taking a couple of steps toward him and then stopping—then a few more steps and stopping.

Finally, they had surrounded him. He ended their curiosity by turning and facing her with bulging eyes, yelling, "Yo, will you all just get the fuck away from me!"

He then calmed down as they all looked at him like deer in headlights, frozen as they observed his off-putting body language. He whispered, "Ladies, none of you have a chance because I am a grown-ass man who does not mess with little girls."

Still, this redheaded, freckle-faced teen continued to look in his direction, smirking as she sauntered away, as if to say,

"We will meet another day." I laughed as they processed his statement. I knew there was no interest because of her age and his beliefs as a black Muslim. He was opposed to interracial dating but believed individuals had the right to choose for themselves and never denounced anyone who engaged in it.

He saw me watching in amusement and smiled back, shaking his braids from left to right. Abdulla was Casanova. He was used to women pursuing him. He was also used to having the ability to choose his companions. Women old and young would approach him, and he would just take his pick. Telling women like that young girl to go away was an everyday occurrence.

As the night progressed, the crowd went from curious youngsters to disrespectful delinquents with no parental guidance. I remember this group of about five young kids from a neighboring state coming in the club. The ringleader was an overweight, sloppy kid. He wobbled from left to right when he walked. He pulled out a stack of money and paid the DJ as much as a hundred dollars to play his favorite song. Then he bought sodas for all his followers and any thirsty girls around him. I'm sure they added a little something to the sodas they purchased.

Once the DJ played his request, they all ran out to the middle of the dance floor and fed the fish or made it rain by tossing dollar bills in the air. I watched all those dollars float to the dance floor. Spectating juveniles ran to the floor to pick up the fallen bills. Even a few of the bouncers came to the floor and grabbed a lost bill or two.

Now the crowd was getting excited, and the club had more than two hundred kids full of energy and no direction. A song or two later, the vibe started to change. I heard the lyrical violence and bass echoing from the speakers, creating an ominous mood. A group of boys started pushing and shoving on the dance floor as if they were in a mosh pit at a heavy metal concert. One of the bouncers walked out and told them to stop and calm down. Then another one of us, minutes later, addressed it again. Romulus told the DJ to change the type of music to mellow the crowd. But it was usually too late.

The playful pushing and shoving led to the girls moving off the dance floor to get out of the way of potential trouble. Then one boy from a group of kids bumped another boy from another group. At this point, an altercation ensued. Both groups stood face-to-face. It was obvious neither of them wanted to back down, but neither of them, at this point, were willing to make the first move. The two groups began to split into two parallel lines, facing each other like a Wild West standoff.

By now, all the bouncers were tired from working consecutive nights. The staff moved slowly to this growing problem because none of them felt like dealing with it. Altercations like this usually led to nothing more than lip service—a lot of talk and tough-looking mannerisms.

The first to intervene was Billy, the nicest guy in the world with the shortest fuse. He was older than I was and was clean shaven with a thin mustache. Billy was the guy who had put that woman in a choke hold on my first night in the club. He had a Hulk-like build that was rumored to be supported by the occasional steroid cycle.

He stepped between the two groups as the rest of the staff congregated in proximity, waiting to back him up. Billy said, "Calm down and relax."

The portly young man with a small following replied, "Or what?"

Billy did his best to let the smart response go. It was obvious that there would not be a second pass given to these troublemakers. Once again in a nice voice, Billy said, "Gentlemen, if you do not quit, we will throw you out."

At this moment, Billy changed his posture. He had his feet about shoulder width apart and bent his knees slightly. It was apparent that at any moment, his button would be pushed, and nothing other than a wild-kingdom tranquilizer dart would slow him down.

The infantile group of young people moved closer together, as if to establish a united front. Then the group that was against the overweight teenager and his congregation seemed to have joined with their enemies from seconds ago. It was as if they were uniting against what they assumed was the Man.

Billy said, "Fellas, are we good now?"

The heavy teen felt like the Lord of the Flies. He looked at Billy and said, "Fuck you, Gramps! You can't do shit to us."

By the time the *f* sound came out, Billy had already started to reach his massive arms out to manhandle this disrespectful, defiant troublemaker. Billy wrapped the large, powerful fingers from his right hand around the boy's esophagus and put his left hand under the lad's right armpit. He lifted him in the air, waving him from left to right like a pendulum.

This, of course, led to the rest of us ensuring order by grabbing as many of the brood as possible. Kids were spreading apart like the Red Sea as we physically hauled the troublemakers out. There was a long walk from the dance floor to the front door, providing us ample time to grab, drag, and manipulate their young bodies the entire way. Once at the door, we released them and explained to them that it was time to go.

They were furious after being embarrassed in front of all their young companions and, of course, the girls. Then they began to yell obscenities and threaten us. Of course, a few of the more primal bouncers responded, trying to establish dominance in a world of ignorance. The kids eventually got into their cars and drove off. The overweight leader of the teens was in an old Chevy sedan that looked like it had been handed down from his grandfather. It was dilapidated but had brand-new chrome, twenty-inch rims. After they left, we all went back into the club to finish the night.

Once the last song played, we started our nightly routine of evacuating the premises and getting everyone into the parking lot. Abdulla's redheaded temptress walked by him on the way out and said, "I wish you would put your hands on me like you did those boys you threw out."

He laughed and said, "Have a safe night." He was obviously flattered by the attention but clearly not interested.

As the youth got into their vehicles and drove around the parking lot, trying to extend the night, I saw the Chevy with the chrome, twenty-inch rims on the far end of the parking lot. Just then, an arm, with something in the hand, came out of the window. Then instantly, there was a simultaneous flash and loud *bang, bang, bang!* Gunshots echoed through the air. The kids in all the cars drove off immediately. During the gunshots, I noticed that none of the security staff flinched, ducked, or moved. We were all completely cool. That was the first time I realized how unique we all were. Remus, on the other hand, hid behind Rush. Smart move, hiding behind a four-hundred-pound wall of a man. This was also the first time I realized the mentality of the dregs of society, the need for the worst of the worst to ensure that everyone in the club knew they feared nothing and were willing to do anything. This is a dominant characteristic of men who want to establish that they are the alpha and nothing less.

Romulus and Remus hated nights like that but loved the extra cash. However, with the youth raising the bar with their violent exploits, it was inevitable that those nights were about to end. There were only a couple more club nights for the youngsters before it was obvious these events were not worth the risk. In the end, we laughed about the experience, and nights like these created bonds that would last a lifetime but expose us all to some extreme occupational hazards.

## CHAPTER 6
# WEDDING SEASON

The winter and spring had passed, inviting the humidity of summer. The change in seasons had resurrected all the leaves and trees that had been knocking at death's door. Another semester in college was completed, and I was getting that much closer to fulfilling my parents' dream of me graduating from the same college they attended. Working at the club presented no negative impact on my ability to excel as I matriculated through my family's alma mater.

The club was the antithesis of what many would imagine the club would be during the sweltering summer months. There were few summer nights with steam-filled windows from the masses' body heat. During this time, the club seldom created opportunities that could compete with the events at the beaches only a couple of hours away. The beach had half-naked women dancing in short shorts that hugged their curves and blousy tops with v-shaped openings from their shoulders to their navels. The beach resembled the dreams of prepubescent, hormonal youth. The club could not compete with those attractions.

There was a casino nearby that had several elaborate ballrooms used for weddings. Many people consider the indoor wedding experience over an outdoor ceremony to eliminate the chance of nature's elements ruining their monumental day. Like any business, the club embraced these random groups of wedding parties looking for a place to party and, more importantly, to spend money.

I had become a vital part of the security team at the club, especially during the summer months because a few of the guys who were staples in the club had taken their seasonal positions in clubs at the beach for big paydays. These seasonal positions created openings for guys like me to take on different roles.

One night I started on the door in Rush's spot, checking IDs. Rush went to a club at the beach during most summers. Rush probably made a thousand dollars or more in just a few nights at the beach. He perched his immense frame at the door and checked IDs—nothing more! I ignored the beach and took advantage of the consistent money that was close to home. In addition, I didn't have to take a two-hour drive to get to work and then at 3:00 a.m. or 4:00 a.m. drive two hours back home.

During a few of our slower nights, we had a couple incidents that I will never forget. One night we had more staff than necessary, creating room for the extra staff to be relieved of their duties. The club was dead. There were probably twenty-five to fifty people in the club around 11:00 p.m. Remus went home to Massachusetts, so Romulus decided to let these guys go a little earlier than normal to save a few bucks.

This left Billy, Abdulla, and me to hold down the fort. No sooner had the guys who were cut had their complimentary drinks and gone on to engage in some type of debauchery when a white Escalade parked in front of the club. A group of about seven gentlemen came into the club, fresh from a local establishment that used exotic dancers as entertainment. They were looking for places to have some fun and celebrate their friend's last night as a bachelor. These guys were drunk, friendly, and just looking to drink more. Romulus saw them and immediately persuaded them to come in for a free round of shots. He knew once he got them in the door, he could squeeze a few rounds of drinks out of them.

By now, it was about 11:30 p.m., and the night was dragging. Romulus told me to leave the door and take his post at the DJ booth for the night. I didn't realize that this was the beginning of my earning respect. The DJ booth would become my post in the club for years to come. I had finally arrived. My days of mopping floors and fetching glasses had passed.

Soon, we would have approximately two hundred people in the club, making for an OK summer night. The bachelor party stopped taking shots at the bar and engaged in the flashing lights on the dance floor. They danced with a group of women, and all was well. As for the staff, it was clear that all the bouncers were counting the minutes until the end of the night.

I put my head down in the booth to take a breath and regain my focus when suddenly I saw the group of seven guys running off the dance floor and out the door. Abdulla and I ran to the dance floor to find a young blond woman with her hand on her face. She was bleeding from her mouth and crying hysterically. She was unable to close her mouth completely. It looked like her jaw was badly damaged. Her friend told me that the guys from the bachelor party had been trying to dance with them. When they said no, one guy took his beer bottle and hit her across the face with it. I saw the glass shimmering as the lights flashed on the dance floor.

Abdulla went up front to explain the situation, and I took the girl and her friends over to the bar for ice and a towel. We asked her if she wanted us to call for an ambulance, and she said no. We asked if she wanted us to call for the police, and she said no. I asked her if there was anything we could do for her, and she looked at me and yelled, "I just got hit in the fucking face!"

I stayed calm and said, "Listen, I am going to take you over to the owner and give you a moment to relax, OK?"

She responded, "For what? I just got hit in the fucking face!"

After a long night that I could not wait to end, I snapped. I looked at her and said, "Fuck it, then!" I just walked away from her.

Her friend tried to apologize for her, and I nodded and just kept walking. Her friends took her to the hospital after providing Romulus with her contact information so he could pay her medical expenses.

The night ended, and I will never forget stopping for gas and seeing those guys from the white Escalade at the gas station. I called Romulus and explained to him that the guys from the bachelor party were right there at the gas station at this very moment. I asked, "Do you want to call the police, or just let it go?"

He told me," Let it go." He was always worried about repercussions from the community. A story like that could cause unwanted negative attention.

As tired as I was, as annoyed as that girl had made me, I still felt that she should have the opportunity for justice. That was why I called Romulus. It was also, like, two thirty in the morning, and I was ready to go home. I did just that. This was another night that depicted how the dysfunctional and inebriated could ruin a good time for others.

## CHAPTER 7
# THE BACHELOR PARTY BRAWL

That first night with bachelor party drama set the awareness for another night with a similar incident. The night was slow, and a group of groomsmen came into the bar early. They were the only ones in the club. Then, a few random individuals came in to get a quick drink. There were no familiar faces. The staff once again was limited, with the expectation that there would not be many people coming out to the club. The expectation of having a busy summer night is always low.

It was still early when Remus and Romulus decided to cut the extra staff to save a few dollars. My first comment was, "Are you sure you want to cut some of the staff this early?" They assumed everything would be fine. I wondered if that was because they had Abdulla, Billy, and me working or if it was strictly financial.

One of the groomsmen had on a shirt with a New York sports team on it. Being from Jersey, I would go up to New

York on occasion. I was curious if they really were from New York. I asked them if they were and started a conversation. The one guy said, "Yeah, I'm from Queens." I had thought he might be because of his accent when he talked to the bartenders. He would refer to them as "Ma" and an *a* replacing the *er* sound in most words. He asked for a drink by saying, "Yo, Ma, can I get anotha?"

He took out a pack of cigarettes and put one in his mouth while he looked for his lighter. We quickly explained that he wasn't allowed to smoke inside any establishment in this state. Delaware had just banned smoking in most public places. He said, "Really?" Then he looked around the bar and realized we did not have any ashtrays out.

I explained, "Sir, if you would like to smoke, you will need to step outside."

He paused as if he were contemplating taking a walk outside and then said, "You know what? After what I have been through with cigarettes, I really shouldn't be smoking anyway."

I said, "What happened to you that would make you feel like quitting smoking?"

He started talking about how cigarettes were part of the reason he was getting divorced. Dennis and I introduced ourselves, and I continued to listen to his story.

He said, "Listen, man, it all started with a party at my boss's crib." His friends all took off outside for a smoke as soon as he spoke those words. They seemed to be irritated that this had come up while they were out celebrating their friend's nuptials. I assumed that they had heard this story before and did not feel like hearing it again.

Dennis explained that he worked construction and the business owner, Mr. Livingston, lived in a beautiful home filled with granite counters and antique furniture his wife had picked out. He said, "My soon-to-be ex-wife had her own business doing interior design in the city." Dennis went on about being a good employee and Mrs. Livingston's interest in interior design. This led to an invitation for them to go to the Livingstons' home for dinner. Mrs. Livingston wanted advice on how to make some of her new decorating ideas work in her home.

This dinner was like any other dinner. They drank, ate, and talked about everything from politics to sports. Then after dinner, they all went outside for a smoke. Dennis's wife and Mrs. Livingston started talking about interior design. This discussion led to the women wandering through this fortress of a home, discussing design ideas. While the women were gone, the men discussed business. Mr. Livingston explained that there might be a promotional opportunity for Dennis in the company. Of course, Dennis was interested. By the end of the night, Dennis's wife had exchanged numbers with both Mr. and Mrs. Livingston. The plan was for her to present design ideas for their house to Mrs. Livingston and then workout the financing of this endeavor with Mr. Livingston.

"Soon after, my wife and Mrs. Livingston started talking and going out regularly. She would say, 'I'm going out shopping with your boss's wife.' At first, I really didn't care because my wife's business was expanding quickly because of the work she was doing with Mrs. Livingston's home. Of course, soon after Mr. and Mrs. Livingston got their home done by an interior designer, it seemed as though the rest of the neighborhood wanted my wife's number to ensure that they were keeping up with the Livingstons."

Then Dennis talked about noticing that his boss had become distant and avoided speaking to him. The promotion that had been discussed at dinner was given to someone else. Dennis figured that he would sit down with his boss and ask if everything was all right. Unfortunately, it would need to wait until Mr. Livingston returned from an out-of-state business trip.

During this waiting period, Dennis's wife's phone vibrated multiple times. He looked and noticed that there were multiple messages from Mr. Livingston's number. All Dennis saw was a question and a couple of statements. The phone texts said things like, "Are you ever going to tell your husband what's going on? He needs to know!"

Now, Dennis thought the worst. Dennis immediately confronted his wife about having an affair with Mr. Livingston. She denied that anything like that would ever happen. He asked her, "Then what do these text messages mean?" She just ignored him and walked out. She got into her car and drove off.

Dennis told himself that he needed to talk to Mrs. Livingston about the text messages to see if she could clear up what was going on. He got into his car and drove over to the Livingstons' home. He thought this needed to be discussed in person and not over the phone.

While driving over, he called his wife's cell. It rang with no answer. He pulled up to the Livingstons' home and noticed that his wife's car was in the driveway. He was furious. Dennis said, "All I could think about was how my boss was fucking my wife."

Right as Dennis was about to ring the doorbell, he decided to turn the doorknob just in case it was unlocked. In many of these affluent neighborhoods, people left their doors unlocked. The door opened without a squeak. Now, he thought he would be able to catch them in the act. He quietly put one foot in front of the other as he went up the winding staircase. He reached the top of the stairs and heard sounds of passion. It sounded like a woman moaning and panting. The sounds grew louder as he reached the door to the bedroom.

He opened the door slowly and saw his wife's head leaned back on a pillow and her eyes closed, enjoying the moment. The sheets covered all of her except her left leg. It looked like Mr. Livingston was under the covers between her legs with his head buried in her valley. Dennis grabbed the sheets as his wife opened her eyes and saw him. He violently pulled the sheet off the bed, exposing his wife—and Mrs. Livingston!

At that moment, he did not know what to say. He looked so upset with his eyes welling with water. So I told a bartender to get Dennis a shot on me. I said, "I still don't get why you don't want to smoke."

He said, "You gotta understand. When I met my wife, she was surrounded by her girlfriends, and I couldn't get near her. I knew she smoked, and even though I didn't at the time, I figured a smoke break would get her away from her friends for a little convo, and it worked. Because of her, I started smoking. It's crazy that a cigarette at a club got us togetha, and because of a cigarette at my boss's house over dinna, it's all over."

His friends came back from outside. One said, "Is the story ova? We all keep telling him that he should have joined in and screwed his wife and his boss's wife!"

The last thing Dennis said to me was, "I appreciate you listening and buying me a shot."

Just then, I figured it was time to get to my post at the DJ booth, but Dennis seemed to be disappointed in the fact that he may never find a good women. His demeanor seemed somber. I patted him on the back and said, "There is someone for everyone," and walked away. Those guys seemed cool, but I sensed Dennis's negative mood might change the group's positive attitude.

A few more guys we didn't recognize started coming in. They were young, loud, and obnoxious. They looked to be from Philly or South Jersey, maybe Camden. It was common for guys from surrounding cities to come to little Delaware and assume everyone was inferior. They never realized that almost the entire staff in the club was from DC, New York, New Jersey, and Baltimore. At one time, I had a friend from Atlanta working with us. This changed the mentality of the staff. We were not local, small-town guys working in the bar. Many of us were in college or had gone to college and were from large cities. A few of the guys were even gang affiliated. We were intimidated by no one and feared nothing. My hunch about these guys from Camden was right. The more they drank, the more belligerent they became. More patrons trickled into the bar. With every addition to the crowd, my fear that these guys might attempt to establish their presence increased.

At first, they made a few friends with the New Yorkers and discussed everything from sports to cars with Dennis and his associates. I don't know what triggered it, but as I was watching from the DJ booth, their demeanors changed. Tension was becoming obvious. One individual with the

Camden group was staring down one of the New Yorkers who was with Dennis. It looked like alcohol and testosterone would be the mixture that created drama once again. They stood up out of their chairs, then inhaled, showing their chests like gorillas or peacocks fanning their feathers to establish dominance. The two guys walked toward each other. I walked toward them, realizing this was getting more serious. As I approached, I saw Dennis notice what was happening, and he got between them, trying to calm them down.

Suddenly, Dennis must have heard enough and punched one of the Camden guys. Now both groups were pushing and shoving. Abdulla grabbed one guy from behind and dragged him quickly to the door, while one of his associates tried to grab Abdulla and keep him from tossing his friend out of the club. Billy grabbed that guy, and they threw them both out. This left me inside alone with about seven guys fighting. I grabbed one of the guys from Camden from behind and started choking him with my large bicep under his jugular, cutting off air and blood to his brain. As one of his friends ran over to stop me, I realized that his body was growing limp from the lack of blood and oxygen. Just then, Abdulla and Billy came back inside to grab more guys and end this melee. They saw me open my arms as if I were trying to reach out and touch the walls on opposite sides of the room. The light-headed patron I was holding hit the ground. He was unconscious. For a second, I wondered if I had held on too long.

I took a step back and asked the rest of these barely legal boys from Camden to pick up their friend and get the hell out. They looked like they wanted to kill me. Their friend started to come to his senses. They watched as one of their own was rolling on the filthy club carpet with tears in his eyes, gasping for air. Reality had set in, and they realized we were serious. They grabbed their friend and vanished as quickly as they had come.

But this still did not end our night. We then had to keep the New York guys from going after them. Billy tried to talk to the group, and I tried to talk to Dennis, but they were too fired up. I thought that maybe talking to Dennis would help, but it didn't. I assumed he had too many emotions built up from his divorce. In the end, we grabbed these guys and threw them out, too.

As we struggled to force these guys out, there was a woman standing by the door screaming. I remember damn near running her over to get these guys out. I hit her with my shoulder and knocked her down onto the floor. How dumb can you be to stand by the door while large men struggle to avoid getting thrown out of the club in an embarrassing fashion?

At the time, I wondered how we could throw these guys out without them coming back into the club. That's when my adrenaline started to decline, and I smelled the aromatic presence of pepper spray. Remus and Romulus had been spraying it in the parking lot, forcing everyone who had been thrown out to stay out. A few had challenged reentry and were heavily dosed with pepper spray, leaving them debilitated. The night ended soon after, but this event led to other problems for the club and for Billy.

The next day, Billy and his girlfriend were at the supermarket when one of the guys from Camden was in the store. Billy recognized him. Then he noticed Billy. Billy told his girlfriend to get something from a distant aisle. He stood by these glass jars of spaghetti sauce as the kid from the night before approached him. The guy made several threatening comments, so Billy took a jar of sauce and slammed it across the crown of the guy's head. The kid looked to be bleeding profusely, but it was hard to tell with the sauce splattered all over his head. The store called the police, and Billy explained that he worked at the club and we had thrown this guy and his friends out for fighting. The local officers on the scene arrested the young man, mostly because the cops called the officers who had been working last night and confirmed the story. That incident made me never sit with my back to the door in a restaurant. I was just like the Western outlaw Jesse James—always on the lookout for the unthinkable.

The other lingering effect from that night came from a not-so-innocent bystander. While Billy and I were by the ramp, forcing a couple of unwanted patrons out of the front door, we bumped into a woman—yes, the same woman I said that I damn near ran over. She decided to seek retribution by way of the judicial system. She filed a lawsuit and said these large bouncers had trampled her with no regard for her safety. She claimed to be physically hurt and unable to go back to work.

Remus and Romulus explained what had occurred to their lawyers and requested that Billy and I have our statements recorded to explain the events of that night. In these situations, the key always was to say that we were restraining individuals and never use words like *choke*. We went into the office and gave our statements. The videotapes displayed a unique vantage point from that night. The owners had reviewed the tape and provided it as evidence to the courts. The case was reviewed and thrown out of court. The woman who had claimed two giants ran her over was caught on tape instigating the chaos. You could see her jumping up and down in the background, pointing and yelling. Saliva was flying out of her mouth on the video recording. She should have been charged for trying to incite a riot or, at minimum, disorderly conduct. She was clearly putting us in danger as we tried to resolve the altercation. The only reason she was by the door was to create trouble. That was the first time that an altercation became a legal problem, and it would not be the last.

## CHAPTER 8
# SLOW SUMMER NIGHTS

I had been working at the club for several months, and my violent antics after the night I choked that patron and dropped him to the ground gave me a unique persona. The larger, more intimidating fellows were so impressed that they began talking about me. They described me as if I were a story that you would tell small children when they were bad. It was like they viewed me as the bogeyman. That's when Abdulla said, "You're always putting jokers to sleep, like the Sandman!" They thought it was a great way to describe me—so they began calling me the Sandman. These fun sessions filled with jokes built a unique camaraderie for us staples at the club. As great as the bonds were between the staff, they did not eliminate those thoughts of being a part of something that fueled the vices of society.

Many staff members did not have the ability to stay. As with most part-time endeavors, the staff overturn was constant. This change in staff brought an old friend back and introduced me to some new ones. One Thursday night, a new bartender walked in the door. I saw that it was a woman, and all the guys were standing around the entrance, trying to assess if they had a chance with her. Out of curiosity, I walked from the dance floor to see who these guys were ogling. The closer I got, the more I realized I might know her. It couldn't be! It was Layla from the restaurant. Her smile was radiant without the metallic covering she had when I met her. She recognized me and came over. That girl gave me a big hug to the dismay of our oversize voyeurs. She knew they were watching, but she didn't care because she was a strong woman who did not get involved in the promiscuous games found in the club. Layla was always a lady. I could hear the groveling over the bass of the club's subwoofers. We talked for a few minutes, and she went behind the bar to start her new bartending gig.

Of course, the goons I worked with surrounded me like flies on shit to find out how I knew her. I explained the story and moved on quickly. Now, by this time I had developed a relationship with the staff, but I did not have many interactions with the bartenders. Of course, one bartender named Melonie asked Layla how she knew me. The conversation made her curious. Melonie had the habit of going to the bathroom as soon as the crowd started to show up. This night, she did her usual routine and vanished into the powder room, and when she came out, I was standing by the door. When she came out of the bathroom, she seemed stressed about something more invasive than the influx of clubbers rushing to the bar for drinks.

She approached me and said, "Hi, I'm Melonie." This was the first time she had formally tried to speak to me. She looked me right in the eyes and extended her hand for a firm handshake. I told her my name, and she said, "I heard from Jimmy they call you Sandman."

She asked me why, and I explained. Melonie smiled and said, "I have seen a few of your moments that resulted in someone being embarrassed. I told my husband about you. He likes to know I'm safe at work."

This led to us becoming good friends. From time to time, we would have a drink with her friends at one of the many local watering holes. She was born and raised in the area and knew lots of people. I met several local bartenders, club promoters, and entertainers through her.

Not long after our introduction, she was fired during the slow summer season because she missed a shift. Remus called her, and she explained that she was at the beach with her husband about two hours away. She refused to come into work, and they terminated her. Her replacement was a bartender who had worked in the club before and was looking to come back. I often wondered if the owners were just trying to make room for him by firing her. I mean, Melonie was eye candy, but this guy was Sam Malone from *Cheers* behind the bar.

This was when I first met Dominic. Dominic was a local guy who had attended a rival college of mine. This instantly led to a dialogue about why each of us thought our school was better. We hit it off immediately. He had a normal build with a small beer belly, and his pants were always sliding down to the point that he needed to constantly pull them up.

Not long after he started working with us, I saw him at a bar, drinking. Dominic always tells the story of this random encounter so it sounds like he caught me out with someone's significant other. Basically, Melonie, her hubby, and I were out barhopping. It was getting late, and her husband decided to go home. Melonie and I drove over to another local establishment where one of her high school classmates was the manager. Dominic always embellishes this part. He tells people that he was sitting at the bar when he saw me walking in wearing a fresh pink polo with the collar flipped up like I was in the Hamptons. He saw me slicing through the crowded corridor and waved me over to the bar. Then he saw Melonie walking behind me and thought he might have caught his high school buddy's wife stepping out with the quiet, angry guy he had just met at the club. We ended up sitting with him and drinking the rest of the night at the bar.

Years later, he told me that, for a second, he really suspected that there was something going on between Melonie and me. At first, he thought he needed to tell her husband, but then he realized it could be a bad business decision to create problems with a bouncer at the club. Of course, this was before he understood we were just friends. We laughed about that encounter for years. He loves telling that story.

Dominic was always telling stories about what he had witnessed working in night spots. He told me tales about the earlier days of the club before I had arrived. He had stories related to scuffles in the club and elaborate tales of how he and his roommates would party after work. The craziest after-party story involved two of his roommates and a girl named Victoria. Dominic said that he came home from work, and two of his roommates had a well-known track star over. She really didn't run track. We just called fast, promiscuous girls track stars. This one was infamous in the community for her sexual antics. Dominic explained that one of his roommates had a problem with sharing, which will be the twist in this story.

Imagine this: both guys are sitting on the couch with this girl. She starts kissing one of them on the lips and then kisses the other. This crazy make-out session turns into these guys calling time out and having a sidebar to establish some rules if they were going to engage in the group thing. The rules were, like, out of the movie *Ghostbusters*. All they talked about was not crossing the streams. Once they agreed upon the rules, they escorted this drunken damsel into one of their bedrooms.

They keep the lights out, and the guys stand apart from each other. One is by the bed, and the other is by the bedroom door. She stands between them and kicks off one of her heels. The stiletto lands by the roommate at the door. Next, she takes the other heel and tosses it toward the other roommate by the bed but misses and hits the lamp on the nightstand. She has on a one-piece black dress. She simply slides one strap over her shoulder and then does the same to the other. The garment slides straight down to her feet. To their surprise, Victoria has on nothing underneath. She takes a few long strides toward the bed and kneels on the edge of the bed, exposing not one but two cavities with an arch in her back. She extends her left hand, raises her index finger, and curls it forward and back, indicating that she wants the roommate by the bed to come over and stand in front of her. He reluctantly goes toward her, and she unbuckles his pants and begins performing fellatio.

As he starts to enjoy the intense friction from her lips, she stops. She looks over her shoulder at the other roommate by the door behind her and waves her hand, inviting him to participate. He walks over with a smile as wide as the Grand Canyon. He immediately drops his trousers and stands behind her. She bends over and puts her face in the mattress. Then she moves her backside from left to right like a feline in heat. He fumbles behind her, trying to put on a latex prophylactic, and then, eureka! It's on, in more ways than one. He quickly penetrates her as she moans and whimpers with satisfaction. She raises her torso with both hands and aligns her head with the other roommate's midsection. Her mouth is open with her eyes closed. She uses her mouth to stimulate the other roommate's now-flaccid unit while the other roommate thrusts in and out from behind.

While both friends are at opposing ends of this female, they do their best to not make eye contact and to stay out of the other's way. It looks like the rules that they have established will not be broken. While the one roommate is being orally satisfied, he comes up with an idea that can eliminate the uncomfortable feeling that comes with having an extra johnson in the room. He starts rubbing her head while she pleasures him. Next, he moves on to her neck. He continues to run his fingers along the contours of her back down to the concave between her lower spine and buttocks. Then, he makes the most aggressive cock-blocking move in roommate history. He slides his hand from her backside down her thigh, reaches over, and grabs his roommate's scrotum! Immediately, his roommate jumps back toward the door with his mouth wide open and a look of disgust on his face. He leaves the room and tells himself, "This is not worth it!"

The other roommate smiles as he leaves, realizing that this night was made for two, and three is a crowd. She takes him out of her mouth and asks, "What happened to him?"

He smiles and says, "He just can't keep up. Baby, you must understand that I am an only child, and we don't like to share." Then he pushes her head back down and completes their erotic episode.

We told crazy stories like this weekly, especially during these slow summer nights. It was always entertaining. We spent much of the night just trying to raise the bar on one another's true stories. Stud always told some of the most interesting erotic tales. I mean, she told us stories about her gay male friends, stripper friends, and of course, her own personal anecdotes. She said all kinds of crazy things. The most interesting was that if you put some earwax on your finger and then put that finger in a girl's lady parts, it would sizzle if she had an STD.

There is one conversation I will never forget. She gave us insight on something we could only imagine. She explained what it was like for her to be with a woman. Please remember that Stud is a masculine woman who has never been with a man intimately. She always played the male role in her relationships. For all of us heterosexual males, the common assumption was that two beautiful women with amazing bodies would be in lacy lingerie. Then they would engage in a pillow fight that led to kissing like in the movies. Boy, were we wrong. Stud painted a different picture.

She told us she was at a friend's house and an attractive woman she didn't know was there. She did exactly what any man would have done, which is find out her story. Stud then used the approach that she was a nonthreatening woman and became chummy with her. They talked and exchanged numbers. This led to a few dates, and then after a few weeks, she came to the club, and we met Stud's new love interest.

### The Other Side of the Velvet Rope

She was a beautiful woman, just like the others we had seen with Stud. Now, just like many of the guys at the bar, Stud also had some horrid ladies on the side. But her new lady was amazing. She was the one that Stud was going to keep. The night we met her lovely lady was the night that Stud convinced her that they should leave soon because she was done drinking for the night. Stud told us that she was prepared and was wearing her strap-on under her jeans as she walked out of the door. She did that from time to time. When they were dancing in the club, her lady felt the appendage, and while in the car, she wanted to see it. She reached over and unzipped Stud's jeans. Her prosthetic limb popped up like a jack-in-the-box. She put her head in Stud's lap and commenced to bring this fake appendage to life by way of oral resuscitation. Stud told us she damn near ran a red light and almost crashed into a telephone pole.

They got to her place, and they started kissing. This led to fondling as they made their way up to the front door. Stud wanted nothing more than to penetrate her immediately upon darkening the inside of her apartment's doorway. She said that she didn't, however. She took her hand, and they went to her bedroom. They stood in front of the foot of the bed, looking into each other's eyes. She slowly took off her lady's clothes, one garment at a time. First, she pulled off the top, then took off the undergarment that was holding back her hefty bosom. They fell out, jiggling with newfound freedom. Stud tossed the large, cupped apparel to the floor. Stud turned her around, made her face the bed, and pulled down her pants to find that she was not wearing anything underneath. She tugged at each leg to get her jeans completely off. Stud pushed her unclothed body down onto the bed. She was lying on her stomach and then rolled over to her back. She slowly separated her knees and spread her legs wide open. I remember someone asking Stud if this was when she put her finger in her ear so she could ensure the coast was clear. We laughed, and of course, she said that she had already used the earwax test weeks ago.

Anyway, Stud lowered her head toward the *y* between her legs, and her lady put her foot on her shoulder to push her away. Stud was befuddled. Her lady told her that she couldn't wait and that she wanted to feel this prosthetic accessory inside her. Stud stood up and took off her jeans, leaving her top on. She started to move forward and stopped.

Her girl yelled at her, "Stop playing! I'm tired of waiting!"

Stud smiled and said, "You don't want to feel this old thing. I have got something special for you." She took off her vascular replica and went to her shelf of toys. She had a variety of little ones, large ones, ones that vibrate, and of course, the pièce de résistance, the ugly one. She dusted off and used the ugly one only on special occasions. Then she stepped into the straps one foot at a time. She put it on like the Caped Crusader fastening his utility belt before hitting Gotham's city streets. Just like one of the guys, she boasted about how she put in work. Stud told us about how her girl was screaming, how she loved her, and how good it felt. She said she feared she was an epileptic from the way she was shaking.

Slow nights might have been bad for business but were at times the most fun for the staff. During the really slow nights, the owners just closed early. Then they would ask a select few of us to go out with them for drinks. The owners

## The Other Side of the Velvet Rope

bought us a few drinks, and we just hung out. Sometimes we went down the street to one of the bars that had exotic dancers. One place was the typical dark venue with several women trying to convince us that their fathers were sick or they were in college just trying to pay for their tuition. They wore pasties to cover their nipples, and most of them had decent figures with OK faces. Still, this was not my scene; I wasn't paying for anything I could not drink.

The other place we frequented was an old, converted house where the women were just as old. They basically danced in circles on top of the glass bar. It gave the patrons a great vantage point as they sipped beer and looked up at the entertainment. This place was grandfathered, and the dancers did not have to wear the pasties—not like it mattered. We didn't care because we just wanted to drink and hang out. The women in this place were unique, to say the least. They either had tight, skinny bodies with no curves or were thick with their bosoms hanging down to their knees. I remember one of them having a bullet wound; another had what looked to be a scar from a knife fight. She might have had another scar from possibly having her appendix taken out, but it was hard to tell from the rolls in her midsection.

Then there was the greatest attraction that any gentleman's club has ever seen. She was my favorite. Her stage name was Shark Attack. I will never forget the first time I saw her perform.

Imagine this...Remus, Dominic, Billy, and me. The music started playing, and I heard the announcer say, "It's the moment you all have been waiting for...The one, the only, Shark Attack!"

At that moment, this woman in this little red robe strutted across the top of the bar. Her industry-standard clear heels clanked with every step. I asked Remus, "Why do they call her Shark Attack?"

He smiled and said, "Just wait and see."

I assumed that she had bite marks on her thigh or something. At that moment, she threw her robe to the floor and displayed to the entire bar that she had only one arm. That was why they called her Shark Attack. I looked at Remus, Dominic, and Billy in amazement. She was dancing with enthusiasm and confidence. She had an amazing body and a cute face. While they laughed, I was admiring her ability to take something that would deny many the confidence to do anything and make it her way to get paid. She had found a way to make the most out of physical disability. I always felt that women should never make themselves into something to be gawked at, but I still marveled at her ability to use what she was given to get over. I started wondering why she was here, because with her confidence, she could have been anything in this world. We all tossed a few fresh green bills at her feet and kept talking.

Dominic said, "That's a damn shame! She can't even hold the pole and pick up her money at the same time." I shook my head at his statement and will never forget how this unique encounter would inspire me to fear nothing when contemplating taking a chance in life. She was inspirational and helped me put my own issues aside. Any adversity I faced was nothing compared to what she had. I will never forget that night.

The summer gave us the opportunity to make a little money and really bond with one another. Nights of closing early and hanging out turned into us going out on the nights the club was closed. Remember, the club was open only three nights a week. This gave us four other nights to find someplace to drink and have fun.

Remus was the best to go out with on these informal staff outings in the summer. We would go barhopping and do some outrageous things. For example, we would go to a bar without paying cover because of what we called "bar courtesy." That just meant that when local bar staff or owners came into a competitor's establishment, that place would let them in and be hospitable.

When we were out with Remus, he bought us drinks and round after round of shots. After an hour or so, we decided what bar we would go to next. Then Remus would tell us he was going to the bathroom. That meant finish your drinks. Remus had a ritual during these outings of clogging the toilets with paper and then flushing them. He would run out and say, "All right, fellas, it's time to go." We would all shake hands with the owners or managers, telling them how grateful we were for how well we had been treated. As soon as we got to the door and stepped outside the establishment, we would die laughing and find another bar to do it to next. We had so much fun during those slow summer nights.

## CHAPTER 9
# WEDNESDAY NIGHTS AND A TRIP TO THE BEACH

Our favorite night to go out was Wednesday night. We would go to this Mexican restaurant for happy hour and drink margaritas. Then we would go to one or more bars to continue getting inebriated. It would lead to this one place that served fishbowls filled with beer. This bar was one of our rivals. Their bar staff wanted to be as respected as our staff, but that never happened. They were a traditional bar with music from a DJ but not quite a real club like ours.

On one of these monumental Wednesdays, Anthony and I went to the Mexican restaurant for margaritas. This restaurant served them in a large, goblet-shaped, oversize glass. We always had ours without salt. Most people stopped at one, maybe two. Not us! We had four or five of them in a sitting. There was no question about how good we were feeling after few margaritas.

I decided to go to the bathroom before heading to the next place, and guess who I saw sitting with her husband

and friends at a table in the restaurant area? Melonie! I said hello and talked with her hubby for a few before Melonie introduced me to everyone else at the table. They were all associates from her husband's job.

She pulled me aside and said, "I'm bored to death. What are you up to?"

I said, "Anthony and I are about to leave and go to another bar."

She said, "Please take me with you guys."

I was cool with it because she knew all the bartenders, which made our bar tab cheap, and she knew the door guys, so we wouldn't have to pay a cover. The working dinner her husband had brought her to was about to end, so she said her goodbyes, and Anthony and I finished our last drink before leaving.

We arrived at the bar, and just as I suspected, she knew the guy on the door, and we walked in for free. This place was packed from wall to wall. As usual, regulars from our club nights and lots of college kids all mixed in with the locals. We walked through the crowd and got right behind everyone who was huddled up at the bar, trying to get a drink. Melonie waved her hand at a girlfriend from high school behind the bar, and suddenly like magic, there were three fishbowls of beer sitting in front of us.

This place was large, with two long bars on each side of an open dance floor. Melonie went off toward one bar, talking to old friends, and Anthony and I went to the other bar. Anthony knew one of the bartenders on the other side. We were set. I found an open corner of the bar to stand at with my drink, and seconds after getting settled, I got a tap on the shoulder from the bartender. I looked down, and there was a double shot of GM sitting on the bar next to my beer. I looked at Anthony and smiled, mouthing, "Really?" It seemed like no matter what I was doing or where I might have wandered, Anthony found me and sent me a shot of GM.

I don't think that the word *intoxicated* truly describes our level of inebriation. At one point, I was across the bar from Anthony, and I looked over at him, and he raised a shot of GM as if it were a toast. I looked down, and a large shot glass with that brown liquor sat in front of me. I took the shot and turned around to see—it couldn't be—the guy with the skull tattoo from last weekend. He was standing with two of his boys.

Time to flash back to the past Saturday night at the club. That night we had an issue with a few individuals while asking everyone to leave the parking lot. The staff was already walking back from the parking lot when, in front of the club doors, there was some commotion. A group of people with the tattooed guy was arguing with another guy. The closer we got to them, the louder they got. It was as if they didn't want to fight and were glad that we were coming to break it up.

Abdulla and Rush got between them, and they started yelling while slowly backing up in opposite directions. Rush moved toward the three guys and simply asked them to find their car. The one with the skull tattoo on his hand walked toward this decrepit car parked in front of the club. I don't remember the color, but I do remember that it had dents all over it. Unknowingly, I was standing right in front of the vehicle, not really paying attention because it didn't seem that serious. I had already started picking up trash off the ground.

*The Other Side of the Velvet Rope*

Suddenly, the focus changed, and Rush was telling the guy to "shut your damn mouth and get in the car!" These guys started calling us rental cops and asking us where our flashlights were as they got into the car. The one on the passenger's side called Rush everything but a child of God. He stood next to the car with the door open. Before he could fully get into the car, Rush reached out and grabbed him. He lifted the man off the ground, pulled him close to his face, and said in a slow, menacing voice, "You can leave here in several tiny pieces, or you can get in this car and go in one piece."

The guy quickly apologized and hopped into the car. The driver was the one with the skull tattoo. He pulled away quickly and hit me with the side of the car in the back of the legs as I was moving out of the way. He realized what he'd done and sped off. Before he left, I kicked his car, leaving a large footprint on the side door. It was not like anyone would notice it with all the other dings in the vehicle. As they drove off through the parking lot, he had the nerve to give me the finger. I was sure he had seen me but hit me anyway.

Now I was standing at the bar with a large amount of alcohol in my system, reducing my inhibitions to almost nothing. Anthony looked at me from across the bar. I think he noticed that the expression on my face quickly changed from jubilant to sinister.

I walked over to the guy with the skull tattoo and his friends and said sternly, "Aren't you the motherfucker who hit me in the parking lot Saturday night?"

His first response was to say, "No." His two associates wisely fled when they realized who I was. He quickly took a step back and apologized, saying that he didn't realize what he was doing. He explained that he feared us. He knew what we would do to them if his friend kept talking recklessly. He told me about how they went to a friend's house and told her about what happened. She immediately told them that they'd better stay away from the club because the guy he'd hit with the car was not the one he wanted to piss off. She'd said I was one of the coolest but not one to agitate.

I calmed down and said, "All right."

He asked if we were cool, and I said, "Fuck no, but I will let this one go."

Melonie came over to us and asked if everything was OK. Her friends in the bar had told her to check on me. I told her that I was cool. She asked me if I was ready to leave because she wanted me to drop her off at her house, but she lived in the opposite direction I was headed, so I went to find Anthony. I told him that he was going to have to take her home. Anthony was like, "Hell, no. Not me. No, sir!"

The clock struck 1:00 a.m., and the lights in the bar turned on. The three of us were finishing our drinks, and Melonie went to the bathroom. I begged Anthony one last time to take her home, and he finally agreed. He knew that this was on his way home and not that big of a deal. I walked right out and drove home. All I remember was getting home and the room spinning before I passed out on the couch.

The next day Melonie called me and said that her husband was pissed that she did not make it home. I was like, "What are you talking about? Anthony took you home."

She took a deep breath and told me all she remembered was riding in the car with Anthony and asking him to just get her to someplace to sober up. He told her that by this time everything was closed and her house was just a few miles south of his place. She said that she told him to take her to his place just for a few. Melonie explained that all she kind of remembered was kissing Anthony and then later the sweat from his brow dripping down on to her shoulder as they made love. At around 4:00 a.m., she called her husband to say that she was at the house of a girlfriend she'd seen out drinking.

I was a little weirded out by the way she described everything to me. I remember thinking, *Is Anthony some kind of predator?* That thought quickly disappeared after they started secretly dating. This seemed so crazy to me at the time. After people had their suspicions about me messing with her, it was funny to see that Anthony, of all people, actually was doing just that.

She conjured up all kinds of ways to see Anthony. She would tell her husband that she was going out to dinner with her girlfriends, and then as soon as dinner was over, she would go straight to Anthony's place for a rendezvous. Her husband was going to flip when and if he found out!

Melonie confided in me that the idea of cheating on her husband was always in the back of her mind. She went on to explain that their relationship had more issues than I could imagine. The night we met in the club she hadn't been distraught because of the rush at the bar. She was stressed because her husband and she had been trying to have a baby for the past several years with miscarriage after miscarriage occurring. After the first miscarriage, her husband was supportive and comforting. After the second and the third, he became more distant. She knew he was disappointed, and with his desire to be a father not satisfied, there was a serious disconnect between them.

It was a volatile situation I didn't want anything to do with. I really did not want to be in the middle of her issues with her husband or involved in what was taking place with her and Anthony. Unfortunately, one time I did get roped into their debauchery. Anthony asked his friend Kendrick and me to go to the beach. He told us that he knew some girls who might come down to meet us. Of course, while we were riding down to the beach, these girls called, and it was Melonie and her friend Nikki. I was thinking, *Are you crazy? Everybody is at the beach this time of year!* I let it go, realizing that it was not on me. They were two grown-ass individuals responsible for their own actions.

We made it down to the beach and got to a club where Rush worked. We had some time to kill before Melonie and Nikki got down there, so we figured we'd go to a place that would take care of us. I hung out and talked with Rush while he checked IDs at the door. Kendrick and Anthony were drinking and dancing with some girls on the dance floor. I never danced; I just sat at the bar and kept sipping. I engaged in only conversation and people watching.

Soon, Anthony got a call, and Melonie told him to meet her at another club. We said our goodbyes to Rush and left.

The club that Melonie and Nikki were at was one of the largest clubs on the East Coast. It took forever to find them in this sea of people. We caught up to them, and the five of us were talking and drinking. Melonie could see in my eyes that I was disappointed in her and Anthony, but I never mentioned the elephant or woolly mammoth in the room.

There was nothing wrong with having feelings for someone, but like all things, there is a way to go about it.

As the night progressed, Anthony and Melonie got more intoxicated. They also became more isolated and intimate. I don't think that the word *flirtatious* really depicts what I witnessed. I saw how being unable to become a mother had her unraveling mentally. Melonie wanted someone more outgoing like she was and less of a homebody like her husband, but this was a little crazy. Granted, Anthony was the antithesis of her husband, but I could see that this was not going to end well.

While these two lovebirds got a little closer, Nikki was all in my face. I was polite, but I did not return the signals that she was sending me. She did little things, like lean in close to me as if she could not hear me over the music. I also remember her putting her hand on my thigh while we were talking. I kept creating distance between us by getting another drink or going to the bathroom. This made room for Kendrick to have one-on-one time and try to make her his tonight. Now, believe me when I say that Nikki was a beautiful woman, but prior to this night, I'd met a handful of guys who all had intimate stories about her. That was a major turnoff for me. Who really wanted something that everyone has had? Especially when the guys in her little black book would corral every promiscuous woman they could get? At about two in the morning, the male portion of the group got into Anthony's vehicle to start our two-hour ride back to Anthony's house. Melonie and Nikki followed us there. I already knew that I was getting in my car when we arrived and heading straight home. The four of them could do what people do at four in the morning after the club closes.

We arrived, and I said my goodbyes. Melonie and Anthony spent the night together. I found out the next day when Kendrick called me that he had his way with Nikki. Of course, he told me in detail all the kinky exploits of what happened between them. He said it was amazing and that she was a freak in bed. He tried his best to say that I missed what could have been an epic experience. He was really feeling himself until I told him that she had a bad reputation and I hoped he covered his little man with latex. This dude told me that he hadn't. All I could think was, *Are you crazy?*

Soon afterward, Melonie called me and said that Anthony had ended it with her the morning after our beach outing. She was quite upset. Melonie explained that in good conscience, he could not keep sleeping with a married woman. He told her to call him when she decided to move on. Then she dropped the bomb.

She said, "I'm not happy, and I know my husband's seeing someone else. I got confirmation the night that I was at the Mexican restaurant, and I left with you and Anthony."

Then I realized that she did not get drunk that night because she was having a great time; it was because she was upset about her husband cheating on her and the miscarriages.

I asked her, "How do you really know what he's doing?"

She told me that I was not the only friend she saw at the Mexican restaurant that night. She had seen Nikki at the bar before we had arrived, and Nikki said she'd seen Melonie's husband walking out of the side door of a hotel with one of his business associates who had been at dinner that night.

Of course, I asked, "What was Nikki doing at the hotel?"

She said, "The same thing my husband was doing."

Melonie and her husband decided to try to work it out. It's hard to hold a grudge when both of you are wrong. Soon after all of that happened between Anthony and Melonie, Anthony stopped working at the club and began dating his future wife, Cindy. We began not to see each other, but occasionally, we would call to see how things were going. That would be the last time that Anthony and I would go out club hopping. I miss him.

## CHAPTER 10
# THE LAST HOMECOMING

My last homecoming in college was an interesting one. I had completed my summer classes and paid for them with the cash I had accumulated from the club. I was still living in my apartment on campus. I had completed my minor in art education and had only a couple of classes left to complete my major in education. I spent my days student teaching, going to class, and working on campus. Three nights a week, I was standing in the DJ booth, looking for trouble on the dance floor.

Homecoming night brought every local man and woman out to the club to partake in the excitement. Like most college students, they would invite every friend they had to visit. The campus would have no place to park. A sea of people walked across the campus to go from one event to the next.

This club night started like any other night. There were only a few regulars like the misfits and their leader, who still came to the club even after he smacked his wife over the head with his radio. The staff came in one by one. A few of them were under the influence of a cocktail or two. Abdulla, Billy, and I were inside. Rush was at the door. Dominic was behind the bar, checking to ensure everything was ready to go. His friend Mookie was talking to him. He looked like something engineered by the government: he was a massive man. It was not the first time I had seen him, but it was one of the first times I really talked to him. He was affiliated with the hustlers that ran the local scene and probably a few that ran the state. He knew the owner of the gentlemen's club that Shark Attack worked at, and they hung out at the bar from time to time. Mookie would always call people he revered "Cat Daddy."

We thought we would have a minute to talk and relax before the crowd started showing up. We were wrong. Remus called the bouncers up to the front door. Cars were coming into the parking lot in droves. The line was suddenly around the corner. Abdulla, Billy, and I were standing outside the door. We set up a red velvet rope to keep the line straight. We stood outside of the door, letting people in one by one. Rush checked the IDs while Stud checked the women for contraband and used her flashlight to look in their purses. One of the male bouncers who was not there to solve problems, only to grab glasses, frisked the men. This night it was Steve, the accountant. He was a clean-cut guy in his early forties with dark-brown hair and a few gray highlights. He watched us horseplay and have fun telling outrageous stories, but he had never been at the club on those nights when the stakes were high and the crowd was ornery. He assumed the job was easy, not realizing that we were that good.

The crowd outside began to push and make the line lose its shape a little. We asked them to calm down while Rush used his thick thumb to click a counter as every patron walked into the club. This was done to ensure that the club would avoid being over capacity. We were getting close to the point when we would tell those waiting in line that when one person left, another could enter. The line buckled more and more, creating a mass of people out front. The people in line became restless, and they started to push their way inside. Billy, Abdulla, and I stood together and pushed the crowd back. It was becoming a violent situation, but Remus resolved it by closing the door to the club and denying entrance to all of them unless the line was straight. He made it clear that they could all just sit outside. Around this time, the cops we paid time and a half for showed up in the parking lot. This eased the tension, and the crowd subsided and formed a better line.

With the police outside, Remus felt more comfortable and told us to get inside. The club was packed with at least four hundred people; the club held five hundred max. I saw the bartenders, Layla and Dominic, making drinks in overdrive with very little capital shown for it. Their tip buckets were almost empty. On my way to the DJ booth, I stopped and asked Dominic how things were going.

He said, "The crowd's buying drinks but not breaking bread."

I just shook my head in disbelief. I continued walking over to the DJ booth and could see lots of movement by the bathrooms on the other side of the club. I cut through the crowd like the sharp edge of a blade and found Abdulla and Billy talking. They told me to go to the door and get

Stud. I barely heard them over the crowd and the music. I didn't even get an explanation for why they needed her. We came back, and they told Stud and me that there were some girls in the bathroom stall together.

Stud walked in and kicked open the bathroom stall door. There was a girl bent over the commode with another girl on her knees with her face smashed into her backside. Stud might have been gay, but she had no tolerance for her homosexual sisters doing dumb stuff like this. It drove her mad. She hated seeing anyone doing crazy, disrespectful acts like this but especially other lesbians in the club. She grabbed the girl who was on her knees by her hair, dragged her up to the front, and told her to get the hell out. The girl tried to argue and say that she did nothing wrong.

Stud said, "You are a nasty bitch—kneeling on that filthy bathroom floor with your face in that woman's ass. Get the hell out!"

The other girl just walked out, but Billy and Abdulla had fun watching the show. I personally could not fathom what made the people who frequented this club do such immoral acts. Was it the alcohol, the club atmosphere, or just a unique representation of what people were willing to do? I did not have the answer.

We started walking back to our stations when a guy at the bar took a shot and randomly started tossing his cookies all over the carpet. Pink vomit from the fruity shot he'd had attempted to ingest was everywhere. Dominic pointed him out and told Billy to come get him. Dominic asked the gentleman to leave. The guy grabbed a napkin from the bar, wiped his mouth, and tossed it at Dominic. Dominic lived for these kinds of moments. He could have jumped from behind the bar and handled it, but for what? He was a college-educated man with a career. Plus, he knew of a worse consequence for this guy's disrespectful actions. He would simply raise his arm and wave toward Billy. Billy would rush over, and Dominic would simply say, "Show him your work!" Billy would act immediately and ask questions later.

Billy's victims had no idea what was about to happen. He would grab someone in one of his variety of choke holds, and all we would see was one arm flapping in the air like it was made of rubber, bouncing back and forth as Billy separated the crowd, swinging this man's body from left to right. In normal Billy fashion, he would whisper sweet nothings in the person's ear while escorting him out. He would say things like, "Why did you make me do this to you?" or "I got what you need, so you know I had to give it to you!" That was one of my favorites.

When he was done tossing them out, he would simply turn, walk away, smile, and call them a "fun dummy." Like a wrestling superstar, Billy also had a finishing move. He took his flailing victim and personally introduced him to the pavement. All we would hear was skin and bone slapping the concrete. In many cases, the police were sitting right outside, watching the end of this patron's night go from bad to worse. They said nothing, and they would crack a smile. After Billy tossed this young man out into the parking lot, he came back in to see if there would be a second.

The temperament of the night was changing. It looked as if groups of people were getting agitated. The DJ was from a local radio station and started pushing the tempo of the music. The bass created the feeling of intensity. Out of nowhere, I saw pushing and shoving across the club by the bar near the front door. Remus started flashing his flashlight to us in the back of the club. We ran up front, and the crowd separated. Guys were along the side of the bar to the right of the room, and another group of guys were against the wall on the left by the front door. Barstools started flying across the room. All I saw was Steve, the accountant, looking scared to death in the middle of the chaos, with both hands up, calmly asking everyone to calm down as if they would listen or could even hear him.

Next, what looked to be a full bottle of beer flew across the room and landed against the wall, inches above a frightened girl's head. She had both of her hands over her head with her chin tucked into her chest. No sooner had we seen one bottle, than it seemed like cases of beer were raining down from the ceiling. Billy and Abdulla ran over and started grabbing guys who were throwing beer. Then Rush came over from the door. A random chair came flying in the air toward his head, and he caught it with one hand. He held it at his side like a batter at the plate. You could see the fury building from within. He looked over and made eye contact with the guy who threw it. By now, all of us were just grabbing and throwing people out. The police stayed outside, waiting patiently for the signal to clear the club.

After we threw a few guys out in some violent ways, the crowd calmed down. One guy started to yell about who wanted some of him and how he would take on anybody. I ran over, grabbed him, and started pushing him toward the door. He tripped on the ramp and lay on the floor. I grabbed him by his shirt collar and belt buckle. I rocked back once before I threw him forward about three or four feet into the parking lot. He landed at the foot of a rookie officer, who immediately backed up and was amazed by what he had just witnessed. The officers told the last of the troublemakers to exit the parking lot before they were arrested on multiple charges.

The officers always sided with us in these cases. They let us do what we needed to keep order. After this crazy encounter, the night was fine. I remember looking into Steve's eyes and seeing the fear left from watching chaos ensue all around him. He was freaked out. He went from being a regular to just disappearing altogether. He came by once after that night, but he didn't stay long.

Like any night, we cleared the club. Then we ushered the crowd out of the parking lot. We cleaned up and, like normal, talked about the crazy things we had seen. Steve sat off to the side quietly. He was worried that we would think less of him. No one really cared. We knew it wasn't an easy job being a bouncer. Any job that asks people to run into dangerous situations takes a special kind of person.

At the time, I was thinking only about running into some of the guys I threw out of the club in the college apartment complex where I lived. It could get ugly with a handful of angry, drunk college kids and their friends all blaming me for ruining their night. I drove home, parked my car, and stayed in my apartment. I didn't get home until about 4:00 a.m. My night was over, and even though many of the students were still scattered across campus, I could relax.

## CHAPTER 11
# STAFF APPRECIATION

I graduated from college with my bachelor's degree in December. During this time, I was flirting with the idea of taking a position in a local elementary school. They offered me $34,000 a year. Taking a full-time teaching position would reduce my earning potential because I wouldn't be able to work at the club anymore. Once again, I was worried about money because I was moving off campus into an apartment. Plus, Remus and Romulus gave me a raise at the club; they started giving me a hundred dollars a night. That was three hundred in cash a week, twelve hundred dollars a month. It's safe to say that the cash persuaded me to look for another position with the state that would allow me to increase my earning potential but keep more free time to work at night.

I told Layla that I was looking for a state job. Layla was a smart, business-minded woman. Her potential had no limits. She told me to apply for an opening with her at juvenile probation. It was the perfect job for me. All I had to do was complete the paperwork, see my clients, and come to work every day. This job provided benefits and a steady income. I could get paid every week from the club and every two weeks from the state.

Then Layla came through with a second job opportunity and told me to fill out an application. She said, "Come to this address and ask for Ava." I did just that, unaware of what kind of job it was or if I could even do the kind of work they needed. I soon found out that the position involved working for a small business that provided mental health services. They had DUI treatment programs, couples therapy, and services for children. I was amazed when Layla started her own practice few years later.

The position I interviewed for was working with children. I became their new wraparound therapist. The wraparound services were used to help youth who had emotional or behavioral issues at home. Layla did not just help me get a job, but she also provided other guys like Rush the chance to work with her providing therapeutic services. She was instrumental in giving me the opportunity to transition from college student to independent man. Between being a wraparound therapist, a probation officer, and a bouncer at the club, I was earning a stable income for a guy without any real bills from college. I had no college loans, and my car was paid off. However, my parents had always said that a job with benefits was better than a job that paid well. That was why the probation officer position I had obtained was so important. Plus, I knew I couldn't work at the club forever.

The club continued to be a revolving door for staff, and it was time to welcome some new doormen. Anthony was gone, and some others would be leaving soon as well. This brought a new staff member named Blake into the club. He was the all-American kid with a baby face. He was a young, married father and a hard worker. He remembered me from the gym I lifted at because he had worked there for a while. He was the one who told me the members used to say I was on steroids. We all were so impressed with him. I told him to avoid letting this place change who he was as a person and never to take his work home with him.

For several weeks, he came to the club to work and then went home to be the best husband and father he could be. Then one night he went out with us for a few drinks and had some fun. I mean, this kid was barely twenty-one years old, and his nose wide open after showing him our connections that came from working at the club: the free drinks at other bars, the female regulars that looked at us like superstars, and of course, the friendship with local law enforcement, which had its perks. We never received tickets from the police, and we were given a pass when we were stopped for drunk driving.

During our staff appreciation night Blake was really able to let loose. Remus and Romulus would plan an all-expense paid staff outing few times a year. They were great business minds and knew that from time to time they needed to show their appreciation for the staff. This time, they rented a bus during the warmer time of year and took us all out barhopping. Of course, this meant none of us had to drive, and we were ready to get inebriated. These nights started with some pregame drinking at the club. One by one, we all started to show up and take one shot after another. The plan was to leave the club after a couple of hours of drinking and go from bar to bar on the buses.

Everyone was invited to our staff functions, including a few cool regulars.

This staff night started with the guys talking and of course flirting with the barmaids, trying to take advantage of a situation that could present a great opportunity to get some action later. I liked to sit and watch it all unfold.

I knew we were in for a crazy night when Billy, Rush, and I were talking by the bathrooms and were in a hypnotic trance from the club's speaker system releasing a sonic sound. It was nice to be able to enjoy the club without surveying the crowd for potential drama.

The speakers were not the only sound we could hear. A murmur came from the bathroom, saying, "Help. Help me. Please." Now, it did not sound like anyone was in trouble. It sounded more pleasurable than anything. We slowly cracked the men's bathroom door and saw nothing by the urinals. Again, we heard the soft call for help. We saw a hand on top of the last stall. A male's fingertips were gripping the top of the stall wall.

Billy looked down at the floor and saw two pairs of feet. Since we all had no regard for privacy, we walked to that stall and opened the door. Abdulla was standing with his arms up, holding the top of the stall while one of our barmaids was kneeling, orally stimulating him. All we saw from our vantage point was her nodding. He was already drunk and enjoying himself an hour into the night. Of course, we ran out and told everybody. When they came out of the bathroom, we all clapped.

Soon after we all got on the bus to go to the first watering hole. It was a small place with a decent light show and crowd. They had a DJ and liquor. That's all we ever needed.

## The Other Side of the Velvet Rope

When we walked in, there were handshakes left and right. We saw some college kids who came into the club on our college nights. It seemed like we knew everyone, and they felt the need to be around us.

One guy who would come into the bar with his wife was dancing his ass off on the dance floor with every girl he could find. The humidity in the room had steamed up his glasses. He was drunk and enjoying himself. We always thought this couple might have been swingers. For example, one night I turned around with a handful of glasses to take to the bar. I put the glasses on the bar for the barback Simon to clean. I turned around, and this guy's wife was inches from my face. Before I could move, she grabbed me with both hands and pulled my face to hers, putting her tongue in my mouth. I remember backing up and her laughing and looking at me seductively. I immediately went to Dominic, and while he was laughing at me, I asked for a shot of rail vodka to disinfect my mouth. I swished it around like Listerine. Her husband saw it and didn't even care. All I could ever think about when I saw him was the night his wife put her tongue in my mouth.

Soon after I finished reminiscing about exchanging saliva with a stranger, his wife walked in, mad as hell. She saw him from the entryway and made a straight line for him while he was rubbing his hands on this young girl's booty and grinding on the dance floor. Out of the corner of his eye, he saw her coming, but it was too late. He'd tried to duck in time but couldn't.

She smacked him upside the head and said, "Your ass was supposed to be home two hours ago."

Everyone was laughing at him. She walked away, and he followed. He dug his hands in his pockets to find his wedding band while racing after her. He was fumbling with the ring, trying to put it on and walk, but his drunken equilibrium had him leaning. He kept saying, "But, baby?"

Of course, all of us walked right out behind them. No sooner had he cleared the entrance when she turned around and slapped him across the face again. This time she knocked off his glasses and knocked his wedding ring out of his hand. It rolled in slow motion across the damp parking lot pavement and hit the edge of a drain. In a blink of an eye it was gone. It looked like it was going to stop, but when it made contact with the lip of the drain, it bounced up and fell threw one of the parallel bars. All of us cringed and winced while watching him get put in his place. With his head hung low, the husband looked like a dog that had defecated in the kitchen and knew he was in trouble.

He went inside to pay his tab and tried to play it cool like everything was all right at home. We simply laughed and told him to get home before she came back to slap the shit out of him again. All but a couple of us went back inside the bar. Dominic, Blake, and I were still in the parking lot for some reason. I think we went to get something off the bus or to use our cell phones outside. I can't remember. I do remember that drunk, crazy-ass Blake saw the college kid from inside the bar. He was sitting in the passenger side of a fogged-up Jeep. We knew the Jeep. This chick who looked like Fergie from the Black-Eyed Peas owned it.

Blake went over to the Jeep and put his head up against the window to see what was going on. He turned around with a giant belly laugh, saying the black college kid from inside was screwing Fergie in her Jeep. Then he opened the door to the Jeep and started yelling at them while she was naked on top of the college kid. Blake started chanting, "Fuck that snow bunny! Fuck that snow bunny!"

We all watched in amazement because she got turned on and started bouncing more vigorously. She repositioned her hands on the back of his neck and gyrated her hips, pushing down with all her might. After what seemed to be several minutes of voyeurism, Blake closed the door, and we all went back into the club. Once again, we told everybody who hadn't been with us about what we had seen. After our story, the young college kid walked back in, drunk and with a huge smile on his face. We clapped and cheered for him.

A week later, Fergie came into the club, and Blake walked over to her and tossed a condom at her. He told her, "I'm going to fuck you with this later!" She was appalled and told him off. He smiled and walked away. He didn't care because, to him, she didn't carry herself like a lady, so why should he treat her like one? Plus, he was happily married and having fun being young in the club. Ironically, she sought him out at the end of the night and asked him what he was doing later.

He looked at her and said, "I apologize for earlier, but I am not interested." You could see the disappointment on her face.

Now, back to our staff-appreciation night. We went to a couple more bars and had several more drinks. When we left the last place to go back to the club to end our night, I was on the bus feeling drunk as hell. Everyone else was still inside finishing drinks. I had my head against the cool window of the bus in an attempt to regain my sobriety.

Just then, I heard, "Help! Help me!" I turned around, and once again, Abdulla had this barmaid nodding yes in his lap. I sat there, laughing. Her friend was sitting in the seat behind me on the bus on the same side. She was steadily shaking her head in disbelief. Soon, the rest of the staff got on the bus, interrupting the sexual encounter in the back. We went back to the club to sober up before driving home.

## CHAPTER 12
# WOMEN AND ECSTASY

After a little turnover, staff at the bar had become family again. One night the people from the state health department stopped by to hand out free condoms to the patrons walking into the club. One of the workers handing out condoms leaned over to me and said, "I have seen several of these people in my offices getting treated for some things that are irreversible." I will never forget that statement. It reminded me of how unglamorous the club could be and really was. During our brief conversation, the DJ played his basic start-up set.

I noticed a female regular who always danced alone on the dance floor. It was the redheaded, freckled-faced teen from the under-twenty-one nights. She was finally twenty-one. She started coming in early to have a drink and own the dance floor before the club was full. She had a drink in her hand, and she was in her zone. Her hips just swung from left to right to the beat of the music. She usually stayed for a couple hours and left by the time the club filled up.

This night, she seemed different. I assumed that she'd had a few drinks and probably was a little drunk. I was talking to the DJ in the booth, watching her. She was swinging on the pole and just in her own world. She typically did not do this much when she was dancing.

This night had been weird from the start—free condoms at the door and a regular dancing in the middle of the floor by herself like there was a party going on that none of us could see. What could happen next?

Well, Billy's girlfriend came to the club to surprise him. Honestly, most of these guys were seeing more than one lady at a time, but they were smart or lucky enough to keep them from stopping by work at the same time. For example, Billy had a girlfriend but still told Rush from time to time to let some girl in for free so that they could hang out for a few while he worked. Of course, on this very night, Billy had one of his side chicks in the bar when his girlfriend came by to surprise him. Billy knew that his girlfriend hated the crowd on the dance floor and would stay up front by the bar. On the dance floor, all he needed to do was acknowledge her, and he could ride this night out if he could get rid of his side chick.

OK, at this point, I assumed that this night was going to be out of surprises. But then, I couldn't believe it. Several of Abdulla's side chicks start coming one by one into the bar. This just raised the potential for chaos. But my man Abdulla was a player. If anyone could master the art of having multiple ladies in the bar at the same time, it would be him. But tonight felt different. Lately, Abdulla seemed to be a little stressed from being Casanova. I decided to survey the club, and I counted one, two, three of Abdulla's

## The Other Side of the Velvet Rope

ladies trying to get his attention. At one point, all three were standing around him at his post. He was smart and always told them that he needed to stay focused on the floor to make sure nothing happened. He used that conversation to keep them at bay. Abdulla had several tricks like this. Another trick he had was to call everyone "baby." Man or women, he would always refer to them as "baby." He answered the phone with the phrase, "What's up, baby?" Of course, the tone would be different when he was referring to a man, but still, using this constant statement avoided trouble. Plus, I'll bet he did not remember all names of the ladies he was seeing, and calling them "baby" made life a little easier.

Abdulla was smart and played it cool. Soon the ladies all went off in different directions to have a good time. He made it clear that he was not seeing any of them exclusively. It was around this time that one of his ladies ran up to him and told him about something going on in the bathroom. He flashed the light for me to come over. I quickly left my post and came over to him. He said, "Some girl is on the floor in the ladies' room."

We got Stud as usual and went into the ladies room behind her. We saw a girl lying still on the floor with a white foam coming out of her mouth. She looked lifeless. We were told that she had been shaking like she was having a seizure. I moved closer, and I couldn't believe my eyes. It was the redheaded regular from the beginning of the night. It looked like she might have been overdosing on ecstasy or some other drug. I looked at Abdulla and said, "We got to get her out of here."

Abdulla whispered to me, "She can't die in the club."

Stud helped us grab her off the floor and take her out of the club. For a little lady, she was so heavy. She was dead weight. We carried her out to the curb in front of the club and called for an ambulance. A woman who claimed to be a nurse walked over and asked us, "What are you going to do?"

We said nothing and laid her down on the curb while the manager stood over her with Rush.

She said, "You can't just leave her there!"

I said, "Listen, we will call nine-one-one, and we have a cold, wet towel coming out for her forehead."

The girl slowly started to move and become conscious.

We got inside, and the fireworks started to fly between the staff and their ladies. Across the bar, I saw Abdulla talking to these girls one by one and them walking swiftly out of the club. Then Billy's girlfriend saw him talking to his other companion and simply left. She knew what Billy was doing and whom he was doing it with. She had just wanted confirmation. She went back to their place and started packing.

The night was over, and we had just started cleaning up inside the club. Before I could get outside to pick up garbage in the parking lot, I heard screeching tires coming from outside. A car zoomed by and almost hit Abdulla.

One of his ladies was screaming out the driver's side window. "I can't believe you got me pregnant and two other chicks pregnant, too!" She was angry and put all his business out in the street. The girls he was dating had somehow planned to stop by the club that night.

Billy's issues were mounting as well. That night, Billy left early to figure out if his girlfriend was done with him and if he was just going to make his side lady his main one. It's amazing how what seems to be the worst night of your life can become the change you needed to be happy. That was exactly what happened to Billy. He left his girlfriend and was finally free and happy with the girl he was seeing. He found peace.

Abdulla, on the other hand, continued his irresponsible behavior and ended up having several babies with different women throughout the years he was in the club and even when his club days were over. I heard years later that he had three different ladies pregnant again, but only one of them had his child. One had a miscarriage, and the other had an abortion. With all of this occurring in his life, he managed to complete his master's degree and went on to complete his doctorate in history to ensure stability for his ever-growing family.

I see him every year at homecoming. He is one of the few people I look for every year. His perseverance in the face of adversity caused by his poor decisions amazed me. He became a great father to all his children but was never tamed by one woman. It was apparent that he was a complicated individual after growing up without a father in an impoverished section of New York City. Even with his faith in god, it was apparent that the influences from his childhood would always influence his decision making.

## CHAPTER 13
# EXTENDED FAMILY

The club staff during this stretch of time had become really close. We started doing everything together. We went to the gym as a group. We partied as a group. I remember when one of the guys found these male-enhancement pills at a local gas station. The Viagra movement had started, and this gas station sold these pills that were kept behind the counter. They were called Man X. Whenever they were mentioned in conversation, we would cross our arms and make an *X*.

One night, we all took them to see if they worked. We played drinking games before work and took a few pills. It was funny to us. We were all at the club, wondering if they really would work. We found out that they worked almost too well. The bass from the speakers vibrated the entire room and everything in it, including us. The pills started to react, giving all of us erections for the duration of the night. It was crazy!

Good times and moments like Man X made us close, but the bad times made us even closer. Some of us, like

## The Other Side of the Velvet Rope

Anthony, had settled down or had become single like Billy after getting caught cheating. Of course, getting multiple women pregnant like Abdulla would be stressful for anyone. All the chaos associated with our poor decisions, the club drama, and promiscuity had brought the chickens home to roost. I, too, had bent Abdulla's cardinal rule: never take your work home.

I said *bent* because I don't feel like the rule was broken in this case. I had seen this woman in the club a few times, but I met her in another bar. She was older and loved chewing this red chewing gum. So, naturally, we gave her the nickname Red. She was also a light-skinned woman, and in some circles, people would call her a redbone. We went out for drinks a few times before I realized she was crazy. Things were fine, and before I knew it, our relationship became physical. This is when Red displayed signs of mental illness from life dealing her a bad hand. After I realized her mental imbalance, I stopped hanging out with her and decided not to be intimate with her anymore.

She would get mad about everything associated with me. One time she saw me talking to a female friend from college in a bar. She was in the bar, watching me, and knew that I had not seen her yet. The conversation between this other girl and me was ten minutes at the most. Then we went our separate ways. Red followed me to the parking lot about two hours later and started punching me like a pro boxer. Then she asked me to hit her back like a man. I had my hands up to protect my face from her swinging wildly at me. I grabbed her and told her to stop it.

When she stopped and calmed down, I told her, "Don't ever say anything to me ever again. If you see me in the street, don't speak. Keep walking and treat me like a total stranger."

After she showed her true colors, the craziest Red story was during one of our college nights. This random college girl was talking about me in the bathroom. The girl was providing a description of me to one of her girlfriends and said, "The muscular one in the hat is going home with me tonight!" I had no idea who this girl was or that she was talking about me. However, Red was in the stall and heard their conversation. She was furious! Red flushed the toilet and opened the stall door. She walked over to the sink right next to the college girls fixing their hair in the mirror to wash her hands. Then Red went over to the hand dryer. Suddenly, Red grabbed a handful of hair from behind and slammed this young girl's head into the mirror. She figured if she couldn't have me, then nobody could. The mirror shattered into several pieces. Her girlfriends were spoiled, privileged girls who had never seen anything like this. The glamour they associated with a night out in the club had become a figment of their imaginations.

Red ran out of the bathroom and straight out of the club. I saw her leave, and feeling of euphoria run through my body. I hated when Red came into my night job. She came into the club to stalk me, and I just wanted her to be banned for life. Just then, I realized something must have happened to cause her to leave so abruptly. Immediately after her departure, this girl with a bloody face came out of the ladies' room. Blood was pouring out of her nose like a faucet. Like on most college nights, there were patrons who were just under twenty-one. Of course, the girl who had her face slammed into the mirror was one of them. The owners smoothed everything over by saying that they would pay for her medical bills. Romulus and Remus let her friends take her to the hospital and avoided calling for an ambulance. After this incident, I started contemplating how long I was going to work in this environment. I loved the staff, but this lifestyle would not last forever, for me or anyone else. Between crazy people high on God knows what and the constant changes in staff, I knew my club nights were numbered.

Like any nightspot, the club continued hiring new staff. We were lucky because many were friends of the current staff, providing an even more family-like atmosphere. There was Pretty Mickey, who was friends with another new guy named Diesel, who had been in college with me but was a little younger. Mickey was from Boston and loved his family more than anything. He was a little older than the rest of us, but he was a great man. The one thing about him I will never forget was his soul rolls. His family had a soulful rendition of an egg roll. He never told us what the family's secret ingredients were, but they were deep-fried goodness. We ate them at every gathering we had.

When Diesel had his college graduation party at his brother's house, I hoped Pretty Mickey would make us some soul rolls for this event. Everybody was going to be at Diesel's house. He was a local and had lots of family and friends. They even contacted some local girls who knew Stud. These chicks would do anything for a dollar and at times for free. I guess they wanted some live entertainment at his celebration. Unfortunately, the party was on a club night. This meant that we would be short on staff from everyone taking off to go to the party. The guys who were working wouldn't get to the party until about 3:00 a.m. I wanted to get to the party earlier because I wanted some soul rolls, and of course, I needed to see what crazy things might happen. But first, I needed to get through a night of work at the club. I needed to get paid.

The night started with me talking to Rush about Simon, the barback, and how funny he was to us. We talked about the night he told me he couldn't date outside his race. Then we talked about another incident when the most beautiful Asian woman walked into the club. She followed Simon with her eyes for several minutes after entering. This beautiful damsel asked one of the bartenders what Simon's name was and was curious if he were single. So, naturally, we corralled all the guys and explained the situation to Simon. He was currently in a relationship with some girl we didn't really like. Honestly, when any staff member was dating someone, we didn't like that person. We were extremely protective of one another. Plus, this girl he was dating was, like, six months pregnant by someone else, and we assumed she was using Simon to take care of her and some other guy's baby. We later found out we were right when she left him weeks before they were supposed to get married.

We gave Simon the rundown on this random gorgeous patron who was the same race as him. We identified her from across the bar, and he just laughed and said, "I have a girlfriend, man," with a smirk. It was honorable, but at the same time, he could have gone from a dilapidated, two-door automobile to a fully loaded Bentley just by talking with this woman. To this day, we think he was crazy and passed on the only time in his life when he could have been with a beautiful woman who also was extremely nice. We tried all kinds of ways to convince him, but nothing worked. At times, he was naïve and gullible but not when it came to doing what he thought was right.

Rush and I continued to talk because the night was starting extremely slowly. This often happened on nights we knew were going to be busy. People loved coming out late at night and then complaining that we closed too early. We continued to talk and Rush told me about the day he met Simon. He said that Simon came into the bar on his twenty-first birthday and wanted to become a bouncer. The guy weighed all of 130 pounds. Rush told Simon that the club was having bouncer tryouts in a week. Simon said, "Great!" Rush explained that he would need to excel in some obstacles, be ready to run, and do some combat drills. Simon left all excited and couldn't wait for next week's bouncer tryouts.

Simon came back in a week and saw Remus at the door. Simon said, "I am here for the bouncer tryouts."

Remus looked at him with a puzzled face. He asked, "What are you talking about?"

Simon replied, "The bouncer tryouts."

Just then, Rush walked in the door a few minutes late for work and saw them talking. He started laughing and pulled Remus aside to tell him what he had told Simon the week before. Simon ended up getting a job as the barback because the camera had recorded the previous one stealing liquor from the storage area.

The crowd started to trickle in, and I went to the DJ booth to talk with DJ Mike. He worked on the nights we didn't have a guest DJ from one of the local radio stations. He was a high-strung, funny guy who acted like a kid with

ADD who had just eaten a box of chocolate chased with a caffeinated cola. DJ Mike was constantly moving.

While working in the DJ booth, one of my many jobs was to take requests from the crowd. I had a pen and a pad that patrons would use to write down song requests. This night, a guy came over, yelling at DJ Mike about the music he was playing. Mike hated that. I told the guy to just move on, but he seemed to be pointing and waving his hands at DJ Mike from the dance floor. I figured it would die down. He was asking for the songs that every DJ would play toward the end of the night. Of course, this patron wanted the biggest songs played at, like, 10:00 p.m., before anyone was in the club.

A few minutes later, these two full-figured regulars came up to the DJ booth to make a request. They were a funny pair. They would put the kids to bed and come out for a few drinks. I secretly called them the Weather Girls, after a full-figured duo that had had a hit song in the eighties. Like usual, we would talk for a while.

Just then, a fight broke out on the dance floor. These two guys were throwing punch after punch at each other. I squeezed between the full-figured obstacles and ran out of the booth. I saw the same guy who had been harassing DJ Mike about the music. I grabbed him and dragged him out the side door by the DJ booth. As I got to the side of the booth, DJ Mike took off his headphones and jumped down the steps of the booth.

I was holding this guy by the side door, about to kick it open and get him out, when DJ Mike punched him in the face. I pushed open the side door and dragged the guy out. Immediately after he hit the patron in the face, DJ Mike stepped back up into the DJ booth, put on his headphones, and continued mixing. He didn't miss a step. That was crazy!

The night finally ended, and we cleaned up. Now we were off to Diesel's graduation party. We pulled up and saw Billy in a black fisherman's hat and a vest with no shirt on. His barrel chest sat up as if he were inflated with air. He had muscles on top of muscles. He greeted us, and we walked into a house full of guys I had never seen before. We grabbed a few beers and went to the basement.

We came down the stairs and saw at least fifty guys standing and sitting around. The girls who would do anything for money were walking around completely naked. I saw them dancing for money and possibly doing other things for a few dollars. Who knew how far they would go? Right after we get settled inside and find a clean spot to sit down two guys started arguing with a friend of Billy's. Billy was probably still outside or upstairs when the commotion started. I ran over between the guys about to go to blows over Billy's lifelong friend.

The tension increased in the room. Pushing and shoving ensued in pockets all over the basement. I put my arm around Billy's friend and protected him from harm. These guys were eyeing me like they might do something. I simply smiled and said, "I don't know who you are, but I'm sure you know who I am. Make a move. What's up?"

They relaxed and let us pass. I took Billy's drunk-ass friend upstairs and outside. I saw Billy, and he talked to the guys in the basement. He found out his boyhood friend had started it with a drunken comment. The noise increased, and we were ready to leave because we figured the police would be here soon.

On cue, we heard the sirens and got in our cars and left. I avoided any police contact, but they stopped Billy. Understand that he was well beyond the legal limit to be driving. The officers that stopped him knew him from the club and let him go. They just told him to go straight home. They even called ahead to some other officers to make sure he made it home. While Billy was riding home with his half-conscious friend, he continued to scold him for messing up Diesel's party.

His friend said something slick to Billy. I don't know what he said, but it was offensive. Something like, "Maybe you need some better friends, and they're not mine, anyway."

Billy pulled the car over to the side of the road on the grass. Billy opened the driver's side door and walked around the front of the car to the other side. He opened the passenger-side door and said, "Get out!"

His friend tried to be cool and told Billy to chill. Billy hit him with several shots to the body. Then he grabbed him, pulling him up to his face, and asked, "We understand each other now?"

His friend confirmed with a nod. Billy pushed him back into the passenger seat. From that moment on, he just kept quiet and passed out for the duration of the ride. That guy was apologizing to the entire staff for weeks after that. His inability to stay sober and be responsible landed him in prison for not paying child support a few years later.

That was so close to being a great night. A few issues in the club made for a long night. Then as soon as we got to the party, a fight ended it for us. To make matters worse, the Weather Girls from the club were in the newspaper the next morning. They left the club and were in a car accident that killed them both. They had children who would never have the opportunity for their mothers to console them ever again. That was the first time that a patron I knew would die on the way home, but it wouldn't be the last.

## CHAPTER 14
# RELATIONSHIPS

Another year had come and gone to make way for a new one. It was Christmastime, and Remus and Romulus decided to throw a staff Christmas party. Of course, the ladies asked their significant others to come out to the party. The plan was for it to be a laid-back event—some food, drinks, and a little conversation. A small takeout place that had been closed for months was next door to the club. The club bought it and expanded. They turned the small addition into a lounge with a pool table and a couple of video games. The lounge had comfortable seats. By comfortable, I mean sofas around the perimeter of the room instead of those hard barstools. It would be nice to sit in the new area and relax like the patrons did while we stood for hours.

The gathering's guest list was the staff and their plus ones. Remus was always single, but Romulus had his wife by his side. Of course, with me being a loner, I came alone. Some staff did bring their significant others, but most came without the extra baggage. Layla brought her fiancé for the guys to meet. He would stop by early in the night but never really stayed long. This was the first night we got to know him. His name was Andre, and I really was never sold on him. Layla was young and very ambitious. She was quickly becoming a businesswoman on her way up. Andre just seemed like one of those guys who would do the minimum and never really be anything but the husband of a successful woman.

Of course, none of the guys brought a female companion. They were always looking to get into something—literally! In addition, after Abdulla had three women pregnant but brought only one new child into the world, it was safe to say he felt like he'd dodged a bullet...sort of. See, Abdulla already had one child. The mother of his latest child also was the only one still seeing him. This led to her getting pregnant again less than a year later.

At this point, Abdulla decided to clean up his act. At the Christmas party, he pulled me to the side and said, "I must change my ways." He told me about how he had gone to the doctor to make sure that his reckless behavior had only given him children as a lasting effect.

I remember asking, "Did you take too much of that Man X?"

He smiled. To this day, I do not know why he chose to speak to me about this, but what I do know is that he was serious, and I assumed it was because of a close call, like he had messed with some girl who had possibly been diagnosed with something that would never go away. Either way, I was elated that he was being a man about everything. Unlike at a previous staff party, he would not be calling for help this night.

Billy did not bring his new lady on this night, either. But Billy did talk about how he was moving out and buying a new place with his new girlfriend. He said that this was serious. He was getting too old to be a playboy and chase women all over town. Then, after laying the groundwork with his relationship update, he asked for a favor. He said, "Can you guys help me move?" Of course, we did, and all we asked for was a case of beer for when we were finished. It was obvious that this night was much different from the previous private club events.

Stud did bring a lady but not her girlfriend to the party. She brought in her young protégé. She was another lesbian that played the role of the masculine figure in the relationship. She was cool. Her name was Esther, and she was a large, full-figured young woman. She had security experience as well. It was nice to have someone who would be on call if we needed an extra hand or a woman to search the ladies upon entry if Stud called out.

Esther and I were cool, but we did have one misunderstanding that changed our relationship. Toward the end of my time at the club, her brother came in the club with a few of his military friends. They walked in, loud and hardly able to stand. Out of courtesy for Esther, we let them in and took care of them. That was a mistake. They became belligerent and started threatening staff. I clearly remember them bragging about being military and telling us how they were trained to fight.

In the parking lot at the end of the night, two of them tried to jump Billy. Billy was grappling with one of them, and then Esther's brother tried to hit him from behind. I ran over and slammed him to the ground. He got up to fight me, and I put him in a choke hold called the anaconda. His cell phone came out of his pocket and was laying on the ground. As he was drifting into unconsciousness, the police pulled up and told Billy and me to let them go.

I got up, handed Esther's brother his cell phone, and asked him, "Did you get all of that out of your system?" He said nothing with his head down still gasping for oxygen. They left, and it was over.

Esther came over to the club a week later to ask what happened. There was nothing she could say because they had asked for it. Nonetheless, I never really saw her again, but I am sure she has no interest in speaking to me. Oh well.

Stud also had brought another gay girl named Sandra and her sister, Evelin. Evelin was beautiful. She had long, flowing, dark hair and beautiful golden-brown skin. Her hair and skin were flawless. The entire night, I watched Diesel and several others do everything they could to get next to her. I knew Sandra from her day job at a local corner store. I simply talked to Sandra while all the other guys used their best lines and tactics just to have a moment of Evelin's time. I greeted her but kept it moving and kept my interaction brief.

I did, however, tell Sandra, "You have got to get me an opportunity to talk to your sister." I texted Sandra for weeks, telling her to organize a chance encounter between us. What I did not do is nip at her heels like a puppy in need of attention like the rest of the male staff.

Because this night was so low-key and we were there simply to enjoying the company of friends and extended club family, I did not realize the ramifications of this evening. This evening marked the beginning of change for many of the staff. I was getting older and starting to contemplate settling down. Thoughts like this did not typically cross my mind. I spent numerous nights surrounded by insatiable woman. The club was no place to meet anyone, especially the one you'd want to spend the rest of your life with. Not that it couldn't happen but I thought it was unlikely.

I did get the opportunity to meet and talk with Evelin. We even dated for about six months. I don't consider meeting Evelin as meeting a woman in the club. What I did not know that night was that she had a little girl and a baby daddy. It was the common story of a woman paying for everything and the man not contributing much of anything. He was an OK father, but as a beau, he wasn't shit. He cheated on her whenever he had the opportunity and then had a problem with her leaving him. They lived in an apartment together, and he was refusing to leave to keep her there with him. She got to the point that her only option to get her and her daughter out was moving. She canceled everything that was in her name, including the lease to the apartment. That made him need to move. She moved in with her mother and Sandra. Her baby daddy knew that he was not going to be able to move in with them. He was forced to move on.

Evelin even worked at the club for about four of the months that we dated. She worked on the cash register. One night Melonie came by the club and said, "I made a huge dinner for myself. Does anyone want a plate?"

I said, "Yes!"

At that moment, I did not realize that Evelin was watching me from the register. I was about twenty feet from her at the corner of the bar, talking to Layla.

Melonie brought the food over to me, and Dominic had been watching everything. He came over and grabbed my hand before I could take the food and said, "Don't you eat that shit!"

It was about quarter past nine at night, and I was starving. I thought that Melonie's timing was perfect because I had come straight to the club after chasing kids on probation and working with one of my clients from my therapeutic job. I ignored him and proceeded to nourish my body.

After I finished eating and Melonie had left, Dominic called me over to him. He told me that the look on Evelin's face was serious when she saw me eat what Melonie had brought to the club. I told him, "If she doesn't want me eating another woman's food, she should cook for her man and keep him full." He laughed.

That was not a big deal for us, but what was a big deal was her baby daddy. He was upset that Evelin had a man in her life he could not compete with. I worked three jobs and had hardly any bills. I was making money left and right. I had thousands of dollars stashed in various locations in my apartment and money in the bank.

This guy even came by the club one night. He stopped in just to see me on a night that Evelin was not working. He was standing right next to me by the DJ booth. I had no idea. I found out later from a mutual friend I did not know we had. His friend told him that he had no chance. I was smart, young, and on my way to becoming something more than he would ever be.

While Evelin and I dated, things were cool, but in the end, she was not used to having a man with the mentality of a provider. I made good money and took her places without her needing anything. From my understanding, she just could not let her guard down after being hurt by her baby daddy, and she dumped me for being a good man. I didn't know how to take that. The day she dumped me, I got in my car and drove to DC to go out with some of my friends from college. My telephone rang the entire time I was gone. She was calling, like, every few hours. I never answered. We did get to talk eventually, but by then, my mentality had changed, and I was done.

This prompted me to create a list of what I wanted in a woman. This list would be the list that would bring Andrea into my life. I simply wanted a woman with no kids, because I did not want any baby-daddy drama, and someone who was ambitious, educated, and cool if things didn't work out. I had seen perfect marriages end with spiteful divorces. Why try to ruin the other person? Just be adults and move on.

Abdulla and Billy had taken turns to change for the better. They had plans to be better men. They wanted nothing more than to make the best of their current situations and remove themselves from the chaos that they had created.

The biggest moment of enlightenment came for Layla. Layla would lose her fiancé because of this night. Andre hung out but said that he was tired and needed to leave. Layla, of course, asked me when he left what I thought of him. Honestly, she could have been engaged to the prince of Zamunda, and I still wouldn't approve. We were all very protective of one another. I simply said, "He seems cool." I had seen him in passing when Layla and I worked together at the restaurant.

I was right to hesitate with giving my approval of this guy. Layla found out later on that very night and every other night, her future husband would leave the club and go see another woman across town while she was at work. The night of the Christmas party was key because Layla met another woman who told her, "I think I know your fiancé from somewhere." This girl was friends with Rush and was there to pick him up because he didn't want to drive drunk and he didn't want it to seem like a booty call. Weeks later, this female came into the club to see Rush and told Layla that she needed to talk to her. Rush's lady friend was a manager at a local hotel and said that she had just left work and had seen Layla's fiancé going up to a room with a girl. Layla was cool about it. She simply left work early and went home. She took his stuff and put it in the middle of the street. Andre tried to make it up to her but couldn't. I even think they became friends, but from her side, it was over. It was easy in some ways for her to move on because he really didn't bring anything other than his erection to the relationship. She had done everything. This led her to dating Lionel, but that story is for a different time.

## CHAPTER 15
# LIVE ENTERTAINMENT AND MORE MONEY

Remus and Romulus did an amazing job of reinventing the club's offerings to keep a steady flow of people coming in. First, they changed the staff's tops from canary-yellow T-shirts to black polos with *staff* in yellow on the back and a small club logo over the heart. They had college nights that offered one-dollar beers from a keg. Bringing the keg into the bar was a unique twist because they typically served bottled beer. They knew that beer on tap might be cheap, but a problem with the carbon dioxide could ruin a keg. In addition, pouring from a keg wasted time that could be spent on serving. Just pop the top on the beer and hand the beer to the patron. Fast service, no wait!

One of the more memorable promotions was when they had rock bands and rappers do concerts in the club. One time a local band came into the bar, and they brought in a crazy crowd. Some of the band's biggest fans were a mother, daughter, and stepfather who would become regulars for a while. They came into the club just for the band. I can still see Rush's four hundred pounds falling to the ground with shock and amazement when the three of them came in the door the first night. What happened was, they came to the front door and saw Dominic at the bar. They were neighbors from a lifetime ago. They were all talking up front. At some point, the mother decided to show them her pierced vagina. Right then and there, she lifted her dress and pulled her G-string to the side to show everyone her piercing. When I saw Rush's massive body rolling on the floor with a look of amusement and shock, I had to go over and see what was going on.

She raised up her dress and lifted her left leg, putting her foot on the ledge. Then she said, "Check out my piercing!"

She showed me, and I immediately froze. But of course, I couldn't stop staring at the decorative jewelry hanging from her labia. I couldn't blink until her skirt and leg were back down.

Those kinds of concerts did not pay great dividends. The club made its money on DJs that played hip-hop and dance music. So, naturally, there were times when world-renowned DJs came into the booth. They would be in the DJ booth next to me and made my club experience amazing. I had the opportunity to work one-on-one with them. Some of the guest DJs would bring out every local DJ from within the surrounding three states. All of them would ask me if they could stand in or around the booth to get a closer look at what unique skills were displayed.

One night a rapper from New York came into the club. He was a one-hit wonder who had written a raunchy hit record about ten years prior. The club was packed. I remember that the club brought in a portable stage for him to perform on. It connected to the DJ booth and covered the last part on the dance floor by the back wall. I doubted that he would even show up to perform. The radio DJ performing that night kept announcing bogus performance times to stretch out the night and build suspense.

Then Romulus came over to the DJ booth and told me that he was in the hotel next door and that he would be coming into the club from the side door next to the booth. Romulus stood by the door, and the DJ told the crowd that the time that they were waiting for had finally arrived. We had Diesel and Billy on the sides of the stage. Abdulla was on the floor with a few other staff members. It seemed like as soon as we got in position, the side door opened, and the rapper came in with two skanky-looking females. They immediately ran up on stage together.

His song started playing, and the crowd moved close to the stage to see the show. While he was rapping, one of the females pulled a random, grimy-looking individual on stage from the crowd. We looked at Romulus to get the signal to kick him off the stage or to let him stay. He let it slide. What a mistake!

Soon afterward, the show took a wrong turn. The skanky girls pulled the guy's pants down to his feet. Then we all looked over at Romulus. He had a look of despair on his face. Think about the potential issues with a club having a guy standing on his club's stage in his skivvies. Then the two girls pulled down his boxers! This random guy was bottomless on stage. His hang down was out for all to see. The two girls got down on their knees and pulled out a condom. All the security staff stood there, waiting to see if we would be given a nod to clear the stage by any means necessary. Out of fear of what we might do, Romulus held up his hand to signal us to wait. Then the girl tore the condom wrapper with her teeth and put the condom on his flaccid unit. The rapper continued to rap while all of this was taking place. The women in the crowd were disgusted and just started walking away from the stage. This guy was standing onstage with a Kool-Aid smile, waving his hands in the air like he just didn't care. The men in the crowd waited to see what would happen next. The girls started to take turns giving him fellatio while the rapper's lyrics said, "Put it in your mouth."

Then Remus ran from the front door to the back door to hit the circuit breaker and kill the power. The lights stopped flashing and the music stopped. The rapper and his entourage ran out the side door during the moment of darkness and left in their SUV. We had the DJ play music for the next ten minutes to make it to the end of the night. We ended the night a little early to get everyone out faster. We had a meeting afterward, and Remus and Romulus told us not to say a word about what happened. If anyone asked about tonight, we were instructed to act as if it never happened. The year was 2005, and Facebook existed, but it was not on cell phones like today. In today's world, an incident like that would have been recorded by a cell phone and put on a variety of social media. It's a good thing that technology was not that advanced at that time.

This probably should have been the last time a show like this was booked, but it wasn't. Some young guys came into the club soon afterward and asked to promote a night with a rapper from Philadelphia. With very little expected in turnout for this event, we were understaffed for what was to come. I pulled in the parking lot like always, and the guys promoting the night from Wilmington pulled up right next to me. The night was dead at first. Then more people started to pile in to see the show. We were not packed, but this rapper attracted a crowd that we did not need to have on a night with only a few staff.

The night progressed, and the star attraction's late entry built suspense. The performer and his entourage ran in from the back door of the club in the alley. Ten men ran into the club while one of the famous rappers most revered songs played. None of them were patted down. It was a winter night, which led us to believe that knives and guns were possibly in the club under heavy jackets. The star and some of his posse pushed their way into the DJ booth, and I could not stop six guys from getting into the booth. Then the two guys promoting the night pushed their way into the DJ booth, too. The owner told us to back up and let the night run its course. As more people tried to get into the booth, the bodyguard of the rapper took his 350-pound frame and stood with me to end the rush into the booth. This caused some friction between the promoters and me. They disliked having their friends pushed away.

There was more pushing and shoving between the staff and the crowd, but we did a good job of avoiding losing our composure. With the help of the rapper's bodyguards, we could kept the peace and ended the night without incident. When I went out to my car, there was spit all over the driver's-side window, probably from the promoters that parked next to me.

This experience made me consider my plans for my future. I did not want to work in the club forever. Some crazy things had happened to guys I knew in the industry. One place in a neighboring state that was always recruiting for good staff had a crazy incident around this time. It was the typical bar story. The bouncer had an altercation with a patron. The patron waited for the staff to leave, and when he saw the one who tossed him out, he shot and killed him. Then there was second incident with a bouncer throwing a drunk guy out of a club in Wilmington. As he was getting the drunk guy out, he lost control of him, and the patron fell down the stairs, too inebriated to protect himself during the fall. He hit his head on the way down and died before he made it to the hospital's emergency room. The bouncer went to jail for ten years for murder.

These incidents convinced me to create a plan to complete my master's degree while I was young and still working in the club. I could pay for school with the money from the club. This was a turning point for me. With my plan in mind, I knew I needed to raise more capital. I decided to do what many of the guys in the bar were already doing, and I started taking on additional security work. We worked concerts that radio stations held, we did contract work of all types, and we even worked in other clubs during our off nights. People from other bars were always trying to recruit us.

There was a guy who promoted male revues. From time to time, he brought them to the club. He was a retired male entertainer himself. Remus would have the dance floor filled with chairs for about fifty women to congregate and watch the show. On these nights, the male revue would start about two hours before we opened. This was great because extra hours meant extra money. Rush would work the door, and I would be inside, getting glasses and getting paid to talk to the bartenders.

This night, the main attraction of the show did not show up. The women would have one less oiled-up man to ogle. The story was that the husbands of the groupies who followed the main attraction had caught him and beat him up after a show. This was a real issue because many of the women at the club were military wives whose husbands were overseas. These ladies were lonely and figured they would just follow this male entertainer from show to show. Sometimes the husbands would show up, and Rush would use his award-winning power of persuasion to convince them to wait at home to discuss their issues with their wives' extracurricular activities.

I couldn't blame some of the husbands after one story I heard. Supposedly, a dancer with a full beard picked up a spectator and held her upside down. He stood straight up with her face in his crotch and her hair dangling at his feet. He buried his face in her groin area as he gyrated with her suspended in the air. The ladies loved to be picked up, flipped, and suspended in air. This incident resulted in an excited woman going home to her husband with crabs in her crotch from the dancer's beard. I couldn't imagine how weird giving that explanation to her husband must have been.

With no main attraction, the promoter came over to me and said, "These ladies think you're hot." Then he said, "Do you want to make some money?"

Immediately, I told him, "I'm not dancing."

He explained to me his plan, and I said, "OK."

So, he called me up to the middle of the dance floor, where all the ladies were sitting. DJ Mike was playing music for me, and the ladies were waiting to see what was going to happen next. Of course, a few regulars there would have loved the chance to watch me get undressed. I was wearing, like, three shirts because it was wintertime, and it was cold in the club.

The promoter told the ladies to get ready because they were going to have the chance to take off each one of my shirts for a small fee. Of course, the regulars screamed louder than anyone else. He started the bidding at ten dollars and then said twenty dollars.

For twenty dollars, the first regular came over to take off the top shirt and, of course, grope me a little in the process. She slid the money into my front right pocket. She kept her hand in my pocket a little too long. I felt like she was trying to play a game of billiards. It was a good thing I was dressed to the left, or she might have tried to make change.

The bidding started for the next shirt at fifteen dollars, and the price went up to twenty-five dollars. The next regular took off my second shirt. Then the process started all over again with all the ladies screaming for more. The last shirt came off, and instead of dancing, I stood there with my muscular physique glistening in the lights and from me perspiring from the trauma of being exploited. I flexed my pectoral muscles as the spectators' cameras flashed to make sure this moment in time would last for eternity on film.

The show ended, and I put my shirts back on with the bartenders and Rush cracking jokes and laughing at the spectacle. I ran next door to the hotel to call my mom and dad from the pay phone. I kept my cell phone in my car when I was in the club. I told them the story, and my mom said, "How much money did you make? Why didn't you dance a little? You could have made even more."

I responded, "I can't believe my own mother would try to pimp me out."

I went back to work. The night quickly went from male revue to regular club. Of course, the story of me taking off my clothes was told to every regular and staff member who walked in the door that evening. It was the joke of the night. Even Romulus told me I should have shook it a little to make a few bucks more.

During these nights, most of the women there for the show would leave, but a few of them would stay. DJ Mike would conduct different games in the DJ booth and give away prizes. DJ Mike decided to do a sexy panty contest. I never really paid any attention to the antics in the DJ booth during these contests. The ladies would line up at the booth entrance, and I would let them in one by one. DJ Mike would be twenty times more animated during these contests.

One of the ladies who was at the male revue came into the booth. DJ Mike grabbed my arm and said, "Did you see that? Sandman, tell me you saw that!"

I said, "See what?"

He then asked the contestant, "Can you show my friend?" He then gave her this puppy-dog look. "Please?"

She said, "Of course." She was wearing jeans like many of the contestants. She unbuckled the belt and then unzipped them. She turned her back to us and pulled down her jeans to her ankles.

I was thinking, *No way!* This woman had no panties on in a panties contest. She bent over, spread her glutes, and left nothing to the imagination in regards to her lady parts. DJ Mike had a face as red as a lobster. He was too excited. She won that night's sexy panty contest.

The night ended, and while we were cleaning, I realized I had made some good money that night and that I should pursue enrollment into a graduate program. Then another opportunity for cash occurred. The male revue promoter ran a club just south of Wilmington by another university and needed some guys to help out on a night that we were not open. This meant even more money.

I went up to the club with Rush to work. I found out quickly why he needed help. The place was very close to the city of Wilmington. This meant kids from the city and the college congregating in one place. This was a bad mixture. I worked there only one night. Diesel was supposed to work with us, but he did not show. At times, he was not that reliable.

I met all the staff I would be working with, but one in particular I will never forget. This was a young white kid who was about twenty-four years old. He claimed to be a pimp. His name was Shawn, but his pimp alias was White Daddy. Shawn—I mean, White Daddy—told me that he had, like, five girls working for him. At first, I thought he was fooling around. Then I realized he was as serious as he was stupid. He told me how he had just gotten this new girl who had given him gonorrhea. He told me that it had been a week since he started his medicine and that he should be fine. Then he offered me a freebie from one of his ladies after telling me about his STD. What pimp offers a promotional quickie after explaining how he just contracted a sexually transmitted disease from one of them? Not like I was interested anyway.

The night came and went without incident, but a few guys tried to start something. Rush and I quickly eliminated that issue. Of course, White Daddy and the rest of the regular staff were nowhere to be found.

After that night, Rush told me that the promoter who wanted extra help did not want me. He said that he wanted the more intimidating guys who worked at the club to come in and work. The next week, Rush went to work up north, and Diesel was once again a no-show. This night Rush was talking to a regular and mentioned to her that he couldn't wait to get something to eat because he had come straight up without eating dinner. She said that she would pick him something up at the end of the night and bring it to him.

Of course, the local troublemakers came in, and Rush had three guys who were starting problems that he had to throw out on his own. The club did have one amazing guy on the door. He looked like a Bond villain's henchman. But that was upstairs, away from the downstairs part. When the situation got physical, the same female regular ran upstairs to get help. Rush and the club's reigning security professional got the three guys out. Rush to this day tells me that he wished I was there because having me would have made that altercation go much smoother. Three on one is difficult for anyone.

When the night was ending, the female regular stayed true to her promise and went to get Rush some food. While she was in the parking lot getting ready to leave to get him something to eat, she saw the guys who were thrown out earlier. She heard them talking. One of them said, "We're going to shoot this fat motherfucker when he leaves." She saw a gun in the hand of one of them in the backseat of the car. She went back into the club, and they called the police. The police found the gun and arrested the guys. If Rush hadn't complained about his hunger pangs, he might have died that night. That night it paid to be a little hungry.

Still looking for extra cash, I had two regular events that I used for supplemental income. The first involved a local DJ who rented out the banquet room at a twenty-four-hour diner. He would come into the club and tell us that they were having a party that night. He then would offer us some money to come in after work to control the crowd. The issue he had was that when the club closed, they would all come over to the diner for the after-party. He needed quality guys to control the crowed.

We would clean the club and get over to the after-party for the last hour or so. We would walk in, and the crowd's demeanor would change. People would attempt to challenge us and say things like, "This isn't the club," implying that we had no jurisdiction there.

I always replied by saying, "Exactly. I am glad you understand we have no reason to hold back here." I could see them pause and process what that meant. They would quickly realize that talking tough was not enough with guys like us.

One night, it got a little crazy. We helped the owner clear out the banquet room, and we locked out the after-party participants. The glass doors provided a clear view of a melee in the parking lot. We told everyone to leave, but they refused. They wanted to watch the drama. The diner owner, Rush, and I watched as the crowd scattered after gunshots were fired. People ran to the locked door to get in, but we just looked at them and said, "Don't be scared now. We told you all to go home a long time ago." They left fast. The police drove through the parking lot soon after it cleared to find nothing unusual.

Most of the time, these nights were great. We would get paid from the club, then make as much as two hundred dollars an hour at the after-party, and of course, the owner of the diner gave us free access to the breakfast buffet to show his gratitude. These extra events helped a great deal with paying for my master's degree.

# CHAPTER 16
# NO CORONA FOR ME

We obviously did accept a lot of offers for additional work, but we also turned down some opportunities. We always evaluated the environment that we were going to work in to avoid any truly dangerous situations. Around this time, I was still paying for my master's degree. I needed all the extra money I could get. Sometimes the money was not worth the risk.

The best example was a female stripper promoter. She was one of Stud's friends. She was a former stripper turned promoter. Her body was ridiculous and unaltered by modern medicine. She was always bringing in groups of woman to dance at a local bar. Her latest idea was to use a bar that was closed and consider the event a private party. Stud said she and Esther were going to work the event to help the girls. The rest of the staff considered working, but the promoter refused to pay us our standard rate. We did ask for a little more than usual, but it was potentially a dangerous venue. Imagine a small club full of naked women and drunk young men! This had trouble written all over it.

The night of the event, we all showed up to support Stud and to check out the place. The bar had recently had a shooting, and we saw that as a red flag. There were other red flags. For instance, when we walked into the establishment, no one patted us down. They patted down only people they didn't know. You're always better off patting down everybody. We walked around and were fortunate to catch the end of the dancer's routine. As the dancer walked offstage, Stud was picking up her money to give to her backstage. The next dancer's set was about to start.

We stood off to the side as the music started to play. She came out onstage and started twerking and moving like a jackhammer. Up and down, the fleshy rump of this dancer went. Her backside was gyrating violently. The crowd was roaring. The money seemed to be falling out of the sky. Before we knew it, she was completely naked. They felt that it was a private party and they did not need to follow the laws of the land. She sat on the stage floor with her hands behind her and opened her legs wide. The guys by the stage in the front row leaned forward for a closer look. Then she grabbed a half-finished Corona. I turned to talk to a friend, and when I looked back, the Corona was gone and the guys in the crowd gasped. Like magic, she had made the bottle disappear.

Bewildered, I turned and asked my friend, "What just happened?" I turned back around, and now the Corona bottle was empty on the stage. Then suddenly, like a sprinkler, beer sprayed from between her legs and all over the front couple of rows. The crowd was silent at this point. They had blank expressions on their faces. Then the onlookers bellowed a sudden roar of excitement. I was so glad I was not working and realized I felt horrible for the cleanup crew for this event. I was disgusted, but different strokes for different folks. I try not to judge people, but I knew I was leaving soon because I could not support events like this. Most of us left after that, and more men came into the bar to watch this spectacle. I briefly talked to Stud and Esther after the event, and they said that the girl we saw perform had been scared to get onstage.

I looked at them and said, "I can't imagine what she would have done if she was comfortable." I was really disgusted, but I didn't let Stud or anyone else know that.

The day after the event, the newspapers reported another shooting at the bar where we refused to work because the promoter was too cheap to pay us. That payday was his last because the local community made sure that the bar was closed for good. It was easy to convince the community to end this bar's existence because there had been several shootings and fights. That crazy night, someone was shot and would have died if not for quick medical attention.

## CHAPTER 17

# RACE WEEKEND

Race weekend was always an epic event. This occurred twice a year when NASCAR would come to Dover, bringing thousands of fans. These weekends were easy ways to make extra cash. The club would open early on Friday and Saturday to accommodate the visiting fans. This meant extra hours that translated into more money. I would sometimes have to wear what I called the throwback yellow staff shirt. This typically would happen because my new black polo staff shirts were dirty. The most memorable race weekend was my last. We had our regular crowd and, of course, the vast number of race fans that came to partake in the festivities.

The Friday shift for me started around six or seven o'clock. I got to work early, and the club had all kinds of race paraphernalia hanging across the entryway, and the ceiling had banners everywhere inside. The club was a giant advertisement. I remember this specific weekend because Horse came into the club soon after I arrived. We had just opened, and a few guys were sitting around the bar, watching television. Then Horse came stumbling into the club. He was obviously drunk. I walked over, and he recognized me immediately. I told Remus that this was the guy who had given me my first bouncing job. We shook hands and embraced before I bought him a drink.

He immediately asked, "Why did you suddenly disappear?"

I explained to him the owner's racist rant. I made it clear that this was the reason I had decided to leave and never return. He understood.

Horse then asked, "Why didn't you tell me?"

I said, "I just knew I had to move on. I ended up working here soon after I left."

We talked for a few minutes. Before I knew it, it was time to get back to work. I walked away and started patrolling the club for empty glasses.

About this time, Layla came in, and she saw Horse. They talked for a few. They remembered each other from the bar. A couple times during Horse's visit, he got a little rowdy, and Remus told me to calm him down. I did just that, and soon he left. That was the last time I saw him.

Friday nights on race weekend always started a little slowly because many of the race fans were still preparing for a wild weekend. They brought campers and lived it up on the campgrounds. This night, about thirty men were in the bar, and this girl who was a local stripper started dancing on the pole in the back of the club. She was wearing short shorts and a tight, see-through white shirt with a popular beer logo written in blue on it. The guys started to get up from the bar to get a closer look at the tantalizing female swinging her hips from side to side on the pole. I looked at Remus, and he gave me the thumbs up to let it ride.

She started taking off her clothes, and every sexually deprived man within one hundred feet came over to toss money on the stage. She did not have much on to begin with, but what she did have on lasted for only a little while. Soon, the chill of the air conditioner was apparent by the large lumps under her tank top starting to push through. She started dancing around me onstage and at one point grabbed me by the back of the head so she could slam my face into her medically enhanced cleavage. That move received applause, and a last flurry of dollars hit the stage.

A few minutes later, I got the signal to end the show. The out-of-towners looked disappointed as they walked back to their seats at the bar, and she took her money. She finished her drink and moments later was gone. She waved at Romulus and Remus as she sashayed passed Abdulla and Rush, who were checking IDs by the front door.

After she left, a drunk race fan approached Rush and Abdulla at the door with a question. He asked, "Hey, can you get me some crack?"

The fan assumed that Rush knew where the drugs were because he was black. At first, Rush was confused and speechless but quickly devised a plan of how to deal with this situation. Rush wanted to teach this guy a lesson. In Rush fashion, he said, "Of course I can get you some."

The race fan gave Rush fifty dollars for two crack rocks. Rush told him to come back in a couple of hours. Rush assumed that he would never make it back because he could hardly stand.

But of course, the fan came back and asked Rush for his crack. Rush and Abdulla looked at him and said, "I don't know what you're talking about."

The fan said, "Come on, guys. I gave you money."

Rush walked closer to the little man and blocked out any light that might be in the sky with his four-hundred-pound frame and repeated, "I don't know what you're talking about."

The fan realized quickly that he had taken a gamble and lost. It was not like he could go to the police and complain that the bouncer at the door took his crack money. He was angry as hell, cursing at Rush and calling him fat, among other things. Rush just laughed at him because he was fifty dollars richer.

When these Friday nights on race weekend ended, it became important for us to prepare for Saturday's rush of race fans. Saturday was when the big events occurred. Those afternoons started with reality stars from television shows signing autographs in the club and ended with our regular patrons coming into the bar. The staff and I were told to stay near any celebrity guests in case someone did something to annoy them. All the stars I met on those weekends were cool.

Another attraction this weekend was a female adult actress who came to the club to sign autographs and sell her pornographic catalog of DVDs. She walked in with her medically enhanced figure in a small miniskirt and a tight top with a plunging neckline. Of course, she was wearing the quintessential clear heels. I was asked to stand next to her while she took pictures for a price and sold her DVDs. She made a killing. The pictures cost ten dollars, and the movies were twenty dollars each. At the end of her time in the bar, she sat on all our laps and had her picture taken with us. I think Red stole my picture out of jealousy. I wish I still had that photo as a souvenir of that time in my life. It's hard to believe that this was the same woman who performed the sexual acts associated with the pictures on the back of her DVDs.

When she left, we had some downtime, and a few of the drunken couples who had come here for the race started to unwind. One woman at the bar flashed her breasts at Dominic. He immediately looked at the woman's husband, who was laughing. He told Dominic, "My old lady has a nice rack for a chick in her fifties." Dominic took the high road, smiled, and left that one alone. Of course, she flashed him and a few others later.

I walked over to make sure everything was OK. Dominic said, "Everything is fine. How is the master's degree coming?"

I said, "It's good."

Dominic had started his master's degree but never finished. I told him that night, "I bet I will have my doctorate before you earn your master's!"

He laughed. Dominic was and always will be one of my biggest supporters. He was always a positive influence.

Soon the club had a nice crowd, and the fifty-year-old flasher was on the dance floor dancing with a few firefighters. In the blink of an eye, her husband's demeanor changed. I guess she did something that took her flirting a little too far. He grabbed her, placing a hand on each shoulder, and pulled her close to him. They were nose to nose. We could not hear what he was saying, but we were watching closely.

The firefighters were respectful and did not want to start any drama. They stood back, just like we did, and watched to make sure her husband did not go overboard.

She continued to flirt and dance erotically with the firefighters. Her husband came over and hit her across the face, knocking her down on the dance floor. Then he started yelling at her. The firefighters backed up and looked at us. We were walking over to the altercation with a slow stride, trying to hear what he was saying. With his slurred speech and the loud country music playing, we couldn't understand him. She was on the floor, looking up at him while he scolded her.

Billy walked over and told the man it was time for them to leave. He refused and said something he shouldn't have to Billy. Billy grabbed him around the shoulders and neck. The patron's feet were off the ground. Billy took him out of the front door with his feet hovering above the ground. As usual, we heard him whispering in the ear of his victim. "So, you like hitting women, huh?"

Once over the threshold of the entryway, he slammed the gentleman on his head at the feet of the local authorities standing in the parking lot. They looked at Billy and said, "I know he did something to deserve that."

I said, "He hit his wife inside the bar and refused to leave."

The officers told Billy's dizzy victim that it was time to get back to the campground for the night. We asked his wife if she wanted to press charges, but she said no. They left the parking lot immediately. When we came in, the firefighters asked if we were OK. The only reason I remember the firefighters being there that night was that they became regulars for a few weeks before being arrested for arson. These guys were starting fires all over town and then putting them out. That was crazy!

Later, the night got a mixture of race fans and locals. One of the coolest race fans who came in that day got into an altercation with a local idiot. The fan was an authentic cowboy, and we talked with him for hours. We started talking because of the fifty-year-old flashing everybody. This local clubber thought being from the big city would intimidate a guy from the country. That race fan tried to let the things he was saying to him slide and ignored his taunts. I believe he tried to let it go because he liked the staff. But once he had enough, it was obvious. He pulled his right hand back and blasted the local guy with a punch. I started laughing. All the staff had seen it coming and just let it percolate for a little bit. We felt the guy got what he was asking for. We apologized to the race fan on behalf of our local idiot and gave him a drink on the house to ease the tension.

This night brought out all the local bandits. We stood in the parking lot and watched the drug dealers selling to the race fans. We saw the prostitutes selling their goods to anyone who was interested. Most people would not notice these things. Our job was to watch everyone. We saw everything that occurred under the lights and in the shadows. The club was on a main road, and all we saw were groups of people walking in droves. We had to look closely to see the debauchery taking place within the masses.

To clear my mind from all these things I was witnessing, I went inside the club. I could see the local staples had arrived. I saw Jimmy and the misfits with their leader. One of them was a guy named Jerome. He was mentally challenged.

I first met him when I was in college. He loved to dance. His moves were a cross between a break dancer and Carlton from *The Fresh Prince of Bel-Air*. I always kept a close eye on him because I never wanted anyone to take advantage of him or pick on him for being different.

The boys from Wilmington who had promoted the rap concert from hell were in the club. Jerome's moves annoyed them. They threatened to hurt him. I did not like people threatening someone with a disability. Jerome's intentions were the furthest from diabolical. He just wanted to party. I approached them and explained that they were to leave him alone. They basically said, "Whatever."

At this point, our encounters were not the best, and I wanted this situation to come to a head so I could end what they started. I was still pissed that they spit on my car. I talked with the staff and explained to them to keep an eye on these guys. Pretty Mickey and I were talking about it when he told me about some guy he worked with who had just walked into the club.

He said, "That son of bitch was hitting on my wife!" I calmed him down, but with a few hours left in the night, I was not sure how long that would last. I had to talk with the staff about his situation, too. Just in case.

Then the inevitable happened. There was some commotion from across the bar. I could see that Billy had grabbed one of the Wilmington boys and was taking him out the side door by the DJ booth. His friends noticed this and followed Billy. Blake and I followed them, and I saw a tussle happening in front of the hotel. I ran through the doors and grabbed one of the guys who was about to hit Billy. I slammed his head into the exposed foundation at the bottom of the hotel's outer wall. He was out cold. The police were outside and came over. The officer called for backup and handcuffed the one I had knocked unconscious. Then Billy and Blake held the other down on the ground.

The officer said, "Hold him down and do what you want until backup comes." The officer had only one pair of handcuffs and needed his backup to come with their cuffs to secure the perpetrator.

In true Billy fashion, he whispered while giving the perpetrator short punches to the ribs. "So, you want to jump people in the club, huh?"

Then the officer said, "Do it. Don't talk about it."

I smiled and walked back toward the club's front doors. As I walked in, the patrons outside smoking cigarettes asked me, "Are you just going to leave him in mulch passed out?"

I replied, "If he did what we asked him to do, he would be comfortably inside, having a good time."

A girl said, "That's not right."

I told her, "He was threatening an individual who is a mentally challenged and started a fight inside. Explain to me exactly how he deserves to be treated after attacking staff, too."

She remained silent after that.

It was late and time for the local drug dealers to come inside the club. They were having some issues with rival dealers during this time, and we paid close attention to them to avoid the streets spilling over into the club. Regulars always tipped us off about potential issues, which helped.

One dealer was not himself. He sat by the dance floor just looking at everyone. He usually was dancing and having a good time. We did not realize that he was looking at a certain individual. He stood up from the barstool and got in the guy's face. We all left our posts, and by the time we got through the crowd, fists had replaced words.

During the scuffle with the staff, the dealer's leg was mysteriously broken just above the ankle. The bone was protruding against the skin. We picked him up and took him out to the curb. We asked him if he wanted an ambulance, and he said no. We figured this much because he was a drug dealer. Remus was worried that this altercation might lead to litigation. We explained that his profession eliminated that as an option. He never did anything about us breaking his leg. A couple months later, he was in the parking lot and asked me if he could come back into the club.

I said, "Of course you can come back."

He had assumed he was banned. That was not the case with us in the club. Unless you were a threat to staff, you could always come back after some time away.

The night ended without any more incidents. The guys in the front of the club were worried about an issue developing with Pretty Mickey and a guy he worked with. Pretty Mickey was fuming all night about this situation. While we were in the parking lot, he saw him and just took off after the guy. He started hitting this guy out of nowhere with haymakers. He was throwing straight bombs. I jumped in the middle, and Pretty Mickey hit me two times in the head by accident. I was a victim of friendly fire. I backed up and started laughing. I couldn't believe he had hit me during his blind rage. He obviously apologized for it, but it was cool with me. I just didn't want him to get fired. We needed good guys like him. This was a crazy way to end my last race weekend night.

## CHAPTER 18
# TWELVE STAPLES

I was working hard toward completing my master's degree when the turning point in my security career arrived. I had passed up opportunities to become a full-time bodyguard, ignored the chance to work in larger venues running my own security staff, and almost started my own security business. By this time in my security career, I had several connections, and I was already doing side contractual work. Having my own business would have been part of a natural progression. With a bachelor's degree in education and being in the process of earning my master's degree in that field, however, I chose a different path that would provide me with more longevity than tossing drunks out of bars.

A single event made me focus on becoming an educated professional and leaving the nightlife behind. This event made me think about the constant fighting, the scandalous women, and the need to have a career with a future that did not involve me living off my physical attributes. My father's words came to my mind when I thought about leaving this labor-intensive career path.

Dad told me about the summer that he worked with a brickmason. He clearly expressed how handling the bricks cut his hands and how the hot, sweltering sun beat down on him. He said, "That was when I realized that I should take the opportunity to go to college." He did not want a labor intensive career. In addition, he realized what life could be like for him if he were physically unable to continue this type of work. I thought about his words and realized that the demise of the club bouncer is inevitable. Anything that is physical can end in an instant.

One night made me think about my dad's words and reminded me of guys like T from the first bar I worked in. T looked older than he was, had no real money, and would never have the chance to retire. I still remember how awkward it was to hear him say that he worked at a bar but considered himself retired. To me, that sounded like an oxymoron. How could he be retired from bouncing while still bouncing?

The night that changed my life was more pivotal than I could have ever imagined. This monumental night, like many others, started with me wasting time with Rush at the club entrance with my throwback yellow staff shirt on. I was waiting on the crowd to trickle in and force me to go to my spot at the DJ booth. I also was waiting on a woman and her friend whom I had met a few weeks prior.

While I waited for them, a familiar face from my first bouncing job came up to the club's entryway. It was Raymond. He was the guy I had let into the bar where I worked on buffalo-wing nights. I had seen him in other bars a couple of times. We always talked for a few minutes when we saw each other. He was obviously reluctant to come into the club, just like he had been years ago when I met him at the restaurant. I saw him and immediately greeted him with a wide smile. He smiled back, and I realized that he had a radiant new smile. The rotten choppers he'd had when I first met him were gone. I told him to come into the bar, and I bought him a drink. I explained to him that I never forgot the genuine concern that he had had for me after I took that punch to the face.

He said, "You took good care of me then and every time I saw you." Raymond then asked, "Do you like my new smile?"

It was clear by the look on my face that I was excited to see he had the opportunity to get some dental assistance. He explained that a local church had sponsored him and made his new smile a reality.

I told him that I needed to get back to work and that if he needed anything to come see me. He smiled, and I told him, "It was great to see you again."

This night also gave Jimmy the opportunity to work with us, picking up glasses. This was the first night that our prized regular (the sarcastic regular) was given the opportunity to work. Jimmy was a hard worker, but he struggled to pay his child support. He had a cycle of working to make a living and then not paying his support. This inevitably led to short stints in jail. On his first night as a member of the staff, he presented another crazy episode of his run-ins with local law enforcement. We always assumed something had happened to him whenever he went MIA for several weeks.

We presumed Jimmy dabbled in street pharmaceuticals, but he was never arrested for that aspect of his life.

Jimmy told me that he had been out driving at 3:00 a.m. with no license, not because he forgot it but because he didn't have one. I remember thinking when this story unfolded, *Of course you don't have a license, and you're driving at 3:00 a.m.*

Jimmy told me he knew there was a warrant out for his arrest for unpaid child support. He knew if the police spotted him, he would be taken in and processed. I know he thought driving without a license was no big deal because he lived in a rural area that had very few streetlights and open farm fields. Who would see him?

Jimmy stopped at a random traffic light, and a police car was parked on the corner. He tried to relax and wait for the light to change. He kept his head straight, but he kept looking out of the corner of his eye toward the officer. It was the longest light of his life as he waited for the red light to flicker off, inviting that radiant green light to signal for him to go. There were beads of water on top of his windshield from a slight drizzle. He did his best to look natural, but he knew if the officer saw him, he was done. All the cops knew him in this small town in lower Delaware.

As the light was about to change, he saw the officer in the car look over and possibly identify him. The light changed, and he started driving. He looked in the rearview mirror and noticed that there were not any flashing lights. He sped up to gain some distance, and just as he assumed he was home free, he saw the reflection of red and blue lights glimmer off the wet windshield.

By now, he had driven into a barren farm area. The squad car was driving extremely fast behind him. He pulled over. As the police car began to stop behind him, he jumped out of the car to make a run for freedom into the darkened fields. The officer yelled, "Stop, Jimmy!"

He looked back and saw the officer's hand on his gun on his hip. He then assumed that the officer would never shoot him, and he jumped up to get to the other side of a drainage ditch. No sooner was he off the ground than he felt an electrifying fifty thousand volts pulsate through his ass—I mean, literally in his ass because that's where the prongs from the officer's Taser got him. There were two prongs stuck right in his rectum. He fell facedown into a ditch filled with water. The officer cautiously approached Jimmy and saw him facedown in the ditch, drowning in a puddle of water. He was still shaking as the electricity went through his body. The officer had to perform mouth-to-mouth resuscitation to revive him before arresting him and bringing him into the station for the warrant.

We laughed that night, but he alluded to the idea that he thought he was going to die. Of course, he lost the job he had for being in jail again. That was why he was working at the club with us. We liked him and figured that he could use the money on a night that we could use an extra hand.

The night was moving slowly, and after sitting and talking for a few, I checked the time. Like on any slow night, less than an hour had passed. I looked up, and Remus brought over a new bouncer for me to meet. He was a young, tall guy with a muscular physique. His name was Marvin. He seemed capable of being a good addition to our ever-changing staff, but we would find out when the shit hit the fan if he could do the job. We spoke briefly, and I knew that soon the crowd would be trickling into the club. It was almost time for me to get to the DJ booth.

## The Other Side of the Velvet Rope

Just before I started my journey to the booth, I saw a flashing light from Rush. I walked over and realized that she was here, the one I was waiting to see. Her name was Andrea, and she came in with her best friend's husband, Jermaine. They were project managers at a bank located in Wilmington. This would be the first night that we would kind of hang out. She was established, without any kids, and single.

I had hung out with her once, but it was not like a date. Several weeks prior, Andrea had been in the club with her childhood friend Sydney. They were in the club to see Dominic, who was in Jermaine's fraternity. They wanted to have a few drinks. They were sitting at a table by the bar, close to the entrance. Her legs were crossed, and the lights were reflecting off her smooth legs. She had long blond hair and a fit figure. I was putting some glasses up on the bar, wasting time during the middle of the night. After exchanging a few words with Layla at the bar, I started back to the DJ booth. I walked by the table they were sitting at, and Andrea whispered, "He's cute" to Sydney.

Sydney hopped off the barstool and grabbed me by the arm. I stopped and asked, "Can I help you with something?"

Sydney said, "Are you friends with Dominic?"

I responded reluctantly with, "Yes."

She said, "My friend thinks you're hot, and we want you to come to a BBQ at my house."

I said, "Cool."

"I will give Dominic all of the information."

"Cool."

It was so fast that we didn't even exchange names. I talked to Dominic, and he did not know anything about a BBQ.

It was clear that this was probably a spur-of-the-moment thing just to try to hook me up with her friend.

They did have a BBQ, though. Dominic and I went and had a great time. I met her friends and their family. After that day, we talked and the plan was that Andrea and Jermaine would come down to the club on a night when Dominic and I were working. Sydney was out of town for work; otherwise, the three of them would have come to the club.

This kind of date night started with me escorting Andrea and Jermaine from the front door to Dominic's station at the bar. We all talked for a few, and I obviously needed to get to the DJ booth. I noticed on my way the crowd was quickly filling with undesirable males we had previously escorted out of the club for poor conduct. Then, I noticed that many of them were walking around and conversing with one another. I realized that they all knew one another and that they clearly outnumbered the staff. I started paying very close attention to them. I watched their body language.

I walked over to Dominic, Andrea, and Jermaine to tell them that tonight might be a bad night. Dominick asked, "Why?"

I simply said, "We have too many degenerates in here at one time."

Like clockwork, a few of these city boys whom we'd had issues with before started to act up, and Billy walked over to tell them to relax. Then Abdulla pulled another one aside and did the same. They started to point at the staff, and I watched as they talked in small groups as if plotting something. I left the DJ booth and pulled Layla aside to ask her to listen closely to what these guys were saying. She did just

*The Other Side of the Velvet Rope*

that and came over to me at the DJ booth to tell me that they seemed to be plotting something.

I went up front to tell Remus and Romulus to give us the green light to escort them out before whatever they were planning happened. I explained how they had a lot of friends and affiliates in the club. This could cause a problem later. They told me not to worry about it. It was probably nothing.

Once again, I was on my way to the DJ booth, and I stopped to talk with Dominic, Andrea, and Jermaine. I explained the situation to them, and they seemed unaware of the potential of what I was saying. Dominic's friend Mookie was relaxing at the bar by this time. The first thing he said to me was, "What's up, Cat Daddy?"

I explained, and he told me that he had our back if anything happened.

I walked away from the bar and just looked around the club to see if I could predict what this night might have in store for me. I did that from time to time to prepare myself mentally for the worst. Most of the time I did this for no reason because nothing came from it. My issue was at times I was right, and I predicted the chaos before it happened. As I stood there, thinking and looking around the club, I saw the same young, freckle-faced girl who almost overdosed in the club give Mookie a hug and start talking to him.

I heard her say, "That stuff I took really messed me up."

He replied, "Baby, you took too much. You know my product is for real."

At that moment, I just walked away and went back to the DJ booth to survey the dance floor. Then right next to the booth, I saw a man trying to avoid an altercation with another man. One of these guys was a well-known three-hundred-pound enforcer for a group of local drug dealers. The music was blaring, and I could not hear what was said. I came down from the booth and stood between them. The one man walked away, and I turned to look at the big man. He stood there, looking at me.

I could not hear him, but I saw his mouth moving. I tried to read his lips. It looked like he was saying, "Fuck you!"

I said, "What?"

Then he mouthed the words again. I stepped toward him to decipher what he was saying, and he leaned down toward my face. He was much larger than I. I suddenly noticed everyone around us moving away to give us space.

At this point in the night, I was getting irritated, and the crowd was becoming more hostile. My adrenaline was pumping. He said it one more time, and I snapped. I put both of my hands up under his armpits and lifted him off his feet. I launched him into the door that was behind the DJ booth that led into the hotel next door. His back hit the door, and it flew open so the hallway light illuminated the darkened dance floor. His back hit the wall and fell onto the carpeted floor in the hotel hallway.

Abdulla and Billy ran toward the light to assist me. The three of us stood there, looking at the sunken figure on the red, worn hotel carpet. He started to get up, and Abdulla and Billy helped him to his feet. He pulled away, explaining that he did not need their assistance.

He looked at me and said, "I was not even talking to you."

I said, "You looked right at me and said, 'Fuck you!'"

Then he said, "No! I said, 'Fuck him!'" He went on to explain that the guy he was talking to was his old probation officer.

I tried to explain, and then he said, "You don't know me!"

I said, "What are you talking about?"

He said, "I got tears tattooed for fools like you."

Now, he was implying that he would kill me. At this point, he was backpedaling because of the insane look in my eyes. Rage was quickly building inside me. Billy and Abdulla immediately held me back. I never let anyone within arm's reach threaten to kill me without giving them a strong, persuasive reason to reconsider that notion. Ten times out of ten, my convincing came via choke hold. He left, however, and this incident was over. I saw him out in other bars a few times after that incident, and he told me once that he never forgot what I did to him that night. But he said that my reputation was good. People respected me for never trying to hurt or embarrass anyone. I just did my job.

Anyway, I got back to the DJ booth once again to keep a close eye on these patrons who seemed to be plotting something. I saw a few of them right in front of me on the dance floor. But these guys were not dancing. The night would be over soon, and maybe this was just in my head. I hoped that everything that I had noticed was just a figment of my imagination or their plans did not involve the club. Then another group of guys came over to the middle of the dance floor, and an altercation ensued. Billy and I got to the middle of the dance floor to separate the guys. Little did we know that that was their plan—we were set up!

This was a similar tactic that inmates used in prisons all over. Fake a fight to bring the correctional officers to a location and then jump them. We were in the same area at the same time. Billy grabbed one guy from behind, and then two guys from the crowd came out and grabbed him. They tussled, and he ended up fighting three guys in one corner of the dance floor. All I can remember is seeing him out of the corner of my eye on one knee with these guys hovering over him. I saw that Marvin, the new guy, was petrified with fear. He stood and just watched everything. I was right about finding out what people were made of once the shit hit the fan.

I grabbed the other guy. He was about six foot four. He did not realize until a little later that he was out of his league and in the wrong weight class. I bent my knees to lower my center to force him to get lower as well. He grabbed me, and I knew more would come if I did not keep my head up and put my back against the closest wall. I was able to separate his hands and spin around to face him. I was able to clinch the back of his neck with my hands and pull his upper body down to the dance floor. I took one hand and pushed his head down to his feet, folding him like a pocketknife. My head was up and looking from side to side for additional threats. I was able to also put my back against the DJ booth to avoid getting jumped from behind.

Picture this tall man folded almost in half, with me holding his head down in front of me by my feet. My first thought was to drop my weight on the back of his head and slam his face into the dance floor. This would present a moment of clarity for all those drunk individuals who thought jumping me was a good idea. At that moment, two others approached me. I simply pushed the guy I was holding away. He was so scared that he left me and started toward Billy. Abdulla came to help, and of course, guys came out from the crowd and grabbed him. He was in a similar predicament to Billy. He was pushing and swinging to get these guys off him. I could not really see what was going on around me because of my own immediate threats. I had two guys with their fists in front of their chins, ready to fight. I kept moving my head up and down and from left to right like a boxer. One guy got close and threw a punch. He was throwing a closed fist. Many people do not know that a closed fist is a great way to break your hand or your wrist if you hit something hard. I rolled my shoulders and flexed every muscle in my thick neck. I exposed my forehead like a soccer player, and I made sure his fist made contact with the hardest part of my forehead. You could hear the crack of his bones over the music. I remember the breaking of his bones sounded over the club's acoustics like popcorn popping. Immediately after contact, he drew back a crablike extremity, and he was grimacing in pain. He hunched over with his arm bent at the elbow, his other hand holding as delicately as possible what looked to be a hand with several broken bones.

At this point, two men had met an embarrassing fate at my hands. The last man was in front, and I threw a warning punch to give him a clear idea of what was going to happen to him. I looked into his eyes and saw that he was noticeably scared. He saw the fury building in my eyes through the flashing lights. Then out of the corner of my eye, I saw a barstool coming down at the top of my head. I rolled my neck again to prepare for the impact of this blow. All I remember is closing my eyes, anticipating the impact of the barstool. I was surprised that I felt the pressure from the contact, but I felt no pain. My adrenaline was at an all-time high. I had not felt like this since I played football.

I opened my eyes immediately, and I saw everyone stepping back in amazement. The coward holding the stool took a step back. I was furious. He was holding the legs of the barstool. I saw that the circular seat of the chair had broken in half and that the legs of the stool had fallen out from the seat. He dropped the legs and the remains of the barstool. This all occurred in seconds.

Looking in his eyes, I told him, "I am going to fucking kill you!"

They ran out of the side door of the club into the hotel. I started grabbing the guys off Abdulla and Billy. We regained control and started tossing everyone out of the club. The police officers doing extra duty were already outside and started to apprehend the main culprits in this altercation.

A crowd had gathered in the parking lot in front of the club and hotel entrances. In the crowd, I saw the one who had hit me on the head. I took off running after him through the crowd of spectators in the parking lot. We were weaving in and out of parked cars. Right at the point when I was about to grab him with no one to witness, the police pulled up in a squad car and grabbed him. He was arrested. The officer told me that he had him, and he called it in on the radio.

I walked into the club entrance with everyone watching me. I did not realize that the hit to the head was deep and my scalp was gushing blood that was mixing with sweat. I had a yellow staff shirt that was covered with blood from shoulder to shoulder, down my chest and back. I walked into the club to make sure that everything was under control. Andrea, Dominic, and Jermaine saw me from the bar. Andrea asked Dominic, "Is that..."

Before she could finish, Dominic had walked over to me. Dominic's eyes were open wide from seeing the contrasting colors of yellow and red on my shirt. Of course, his first question was not the conventional, "Are you OK?" No! He asked me, "Did you get real mad and finally bite someone in the face?"

I said, "No!"

Dominic explained that he went to the dance floor when the side door opened and realized that he was out there all alone. A guy had come over and asked Dominic if he wanted some, too. Mookie's large frame came from out of the shadows and said, "Do I need to make a phone call? This is my oldest friend, and you're not going to do anything." Dominic said that the kid ran away. If it weren't for Mookie, those guys would have beaten Dominic down.

He walked back to the bar and told Jermaine and Andrea that I was OK. After we debriefed with the police, an ambulance came for me. Andrea waited with me and took a rag to clean the blood from my brow. I can still hear me asking, "How bad does it look?"

Andrea said, "You're definitely going to need stitches."

Then one of the more comical officers laughed and said, "Stitches? You're getting staples."

We went to the hospital. I remember the beeping from the ambulance as it backed into the emergency entrance. I tried to get up to walk in, and the person in the back with me told me, "We must wheel you in because you have a head wound." I got up, anyway, and proceeded to get out of the vehicle. He said, "If you're sure you are OK, go ahead."

While I was in the back of the emergency room, providing my medical information, I noticed that Red was standing in the distance. She had been at the club and followed the ambulance to the hospital to make sure I was OK. She tried to talk to me, but I cut her short and just explained that I was fine. She was content with that and left.

I contacted the club and told them I was fine. After they had cleaned up, many of my brethren came to make sure I was OK. They told me that Marvin left after the fight. He realized we have fun, but when it was time to handle problems like tonight, this job wasn't for him.

I spent the early part of the morning in the hospital, getting my brain scanned because of the visible trauma to my head. This occurred before they closed the wound. I will never forget getting twelve staples in the top of my head. The anesthesia had been applied to my head, but they missed a spot. I took the last few staples one by one without anything for the pain. I can still visualize the overworked doctor's amazed facial expression when she witnessed my tolerance for pain.

By now, it was, like, 3:00 a.m., and I was still pissed. I called my parents to tell them what had happened to me while I waited to be released. I was so upset that someone would hit me with a barstool. I was beyond angry, but my father talked to me, and I calmed down. My mom became more concerned for my safety and took out a life insurance plan on me. My parents knew that I had never been the kind of person most people would fight. You shoot people like me.

## The Other Side of the Velvet Rope

While I was on the phone, the guys from the club showed up. I got a ride from one of them to get my car from the club. While riding home from the club, I called Andrea on my cell to tell her I was all right. She hardly knew me and apologized for leaving, but she had not driven to the bar that night and she had not wanted to hold up her ride. She had even considered driving back down to take care of me, but after drinking all night, it was not a good idea. But she did come over the next day to take care of me.

A week later, like clockwork, I went right back to work. When I saw Romulus, he immediately said, "Send me the bill, and I will pay for it." Remus told me that I should not be working. He went into the office and showed me the remains of the stool that had hit me. Some of the staff wanted me to leave and not work. Remus knew I wouldn't leave, and he just told me not to get involved in any altercations. He directed me to just run the DJ booth, especially after he saw the three-inch lump with staples running over it like train tracks on top of my head.

I saw Jimmy working in the club that next week, too. I can recall how relieved he was to see that I was all right. He started to tear up while we revisited the event in our discussion. He explained how hard it was to watch all of us fighting. He had been forced to sit on the sidelines because he could not afford to take any hits to the head because of a tube draining fluid from his brain. A blow to the head could be fatal. I had never realized how much he loved all of us at the club. After our conversation, we embraced and went to work. Most people after that event viewed me as a legend that you would hear about in urban folklore. I never had to do anything physical in the club after that incident. The fabricated stories associated with that night made people think twice.

CHAPTER 19

# THE END IS NEAR

In 2004, Remus and Romulus were going through a change. They had worked together for going on twenty years in various positions in the bar industry. One night, the signs were there that this partnership might be coming to an end. I remember it because I was dealing with the death of my grandfather or, really, my uncle. My father's aunt and uncle took him in as a child and raised him. They were like my grandparents. I met my real grandfather only a couple of times, but because of his battle with glaucoma, he really saw me only once when I was about eight years old. My aunt and uncle who raised my father, I saw all the time. It seemed like they were all passing one by one every year. For me, it was upsetting, but for my father, it was devastating. Still to this day, I can't imagine losing so many important figures in one's life like my father did. The timeline is like this: his mother died very young, and then his father was gone, then his surrogate parents. It was hard to watch him deal with so many losses.

This is significant because around this time, Romulus lost his father. Romulus and I talked about sports, but we never really talked about anything personal. One night he came over to the DJ booth and started telling me about how painful it was to have lost his father. I could not relate, but I do remember seeing the same pain in his eyes that was in my father's. He mentioned to me in that discussion that he missed home. He was not a local, and honestly, I had no idea what led him to move into this area.

This event created a disconnect between Remus and Romulus. Romulus wanted to go back home, and I think his wife wanted to do the same. This would force Remus to either follow them home or move on alone. Either way, the writing was on the wall. Romulus and his wife ended up moving back to their hometown. He went on to establish his dream of running an even-larger club named Rome. Remus simply disappeared. We heard stories that he owned a club in Florida near a local college, but I never really found out for sure.

Remus and Romulus sold the club to three young individuals they had known for years. They were friends. In the end, I think they paid the so-called new owners to run the club for a fee and still send them a check. They were smart businessmen. They rented homes in the area so that they could leave whenever they wanted. They did just that; they left. I never saw them again.

All good things come to an end, and things were changing at the club. Our legacy as the most infamous, dominant, and respected security team anywhere at that time was deteriorating. Abdulla graduated with his master's degree and moved to a college down south to complete his doctorate. Other staff members started to leave as well, to pursue new careers or get away from the drama associated with the club. It was just Billy, Rush, and me left.

During the short time that I was with the new management, I took on the role of bouncer and bartender. I would bounce when they needed and bartend when necessary. Bartending was OK because of the opportunity to make more money from my tips. I do remember loving the interactions with the patrons. I thought I had learned a lot about these people from my interactions as a bouncer, but nothing could compare to what the drunks sitting at the bar would say. They really felt like the bartender was their best friend and that they could tell me anything.

I remember Layla and I were working the same part of the bar when this regular came into the bar. She had, like, four kids and always had a story. She told us everything. She told us how her stepfather molesting her as a child ruined her life and why she was getting a divorce from her husband, who never came into the club with her. This night after telling us all these dismal tales, she told us about why she came out to the bar. She was excited that her insurance would cover her plastic surgery.

Of course, to make conversation with her, I asked, "So, what are you getting done? Your nose, boobs, what?"

Then she told Layla and me that she was getting a labiaplasty. I had no idea what that was. She then explained that after four kids, her lady parts had been stretched and beaten up. I wanted to be anyplace else at that time but realized she was in better spirits, so I bought her a shot to help her celebrate something positive. Then she continued to elaborate about how the doctor would make her vagina like new. It would be tight, petite, and cute again. I started to get curious and wanted to see before and after pictures. Of course, I did not ask; it was just a thought.

My time bartending and bouncing was about to end because I was approaching the end of my master's program. Andrea and I had bought a house around this time. She was pressuring me to leave the bar for good. We occasionally argued about me being so close to finishing my master's degree and how working in the club was counterproductive. Soon afterward, we would take a trip to Vegas, see a mixed martial arts event, and get married at one of those Elvis chapels. Our honeymoon night started with getting hitched, followed by viewing our first live MMA event together, and ended with practicing for the conception of what would be the coolest little dude ever. Between owning a home together and then getting married, she was becoming more adamant about me letting the nightlife go.

On one of my last nights as a bouncer in the club, I saw Jimmy, Skip, and others from my past. It was as if the universe wanted to remind me of how it all started. Looking back, it was great to see them one last time. This night also brought back a foe from my past. The night I earned my twelve staples, I had thrown out a drug dealer's three-hundred-pound enforcer.

I stood in the DJ booth, and he came over to me and asked me, "Can I stand here?"

I said, "Sure."

At first, I did not recognize him. He had been incarcerated for several months, and he had lost about a hundred pounds. I assumed that his ignorant behavior was a thing of the past. I was wrong. A newer staff member came by me, and the rehabilitated patron gave him a look filled with disrespect. As the staff member walked away, they made eye contact.

He looked at the young guy and said, "What are you looking at?"

I stood there and told him to chill.

He said, "I'm cool."

The club was packed and filled with these young college kids with aspirations of being modern-day gangsters. It frustrated me to see young people with the opportunity to pursue academia reduce their goals to hoodlum activity that they could do free at home without amassing student-loan debt. The college kids from neighboring cities and the local kids at times mixed like oil and water. This was one of those nights.

We had talked to several of them about calming down because they were getting too rowdy. They never did anything worth being asked to leave over, but they were changing the temperament in the club. Toward the end of the night, after various pills had been popped and drinks consumed, we had an all-out brawl. The club was almost divided in half—the locals on one side and the college kids on the other.

Billy, Rush, and I were just grabbing guys and taking them to the front door. Chairs were flying across the room. Girls were under tables and in corners of the club to avoid becoming collateral damage. Billy and I ran into the club and stood on the dance floor, not realizing we were between both groups. The college kids were up by the bar, and the locals were on the dance floor, with us standing between them. Billy and I stood back-to-back. We started pushing them back on both sides. I assumed that Billy and I would be fighting for our lives. It was, like, ten to one. We were overpowered.

Then a hand came over my shoulder and sprayed pepper spray into the air. Patrons coughed and gasped for air. The flashing club lights illuminated the particles in the air. Many were fortunate to make it outside. Some did not and were forced to stay inside with the polluted air. Others were down on their knees, vomiting, and a few were just bent over dry heaving. We helped everyone out and turned on the fans.

Soon afterward, I left the club and retired. I had realized that the end was near, and it was apparent that my nightlife was a stressor for my home life. It was time for me to move on and take care of my wife and newborn son. Everything had changed. The family I had gained working at the club had almost all left, and I felt that it was my turn. Even Dominic had left and started working in a brand-new bar north of the club. It was officially over. I miss those times, all the staff, and those patrons that came in every night.

## CHAPTER 20
# THE RETURN OF THE SANDMAN

Dominic and I were living in the same small town about twenty-five miles north of the club when the idea of returning to the club scene came up. Both of us were married and working as educators. I had almost completed my master's program. Dominic had an old bar friend who opened his own restaurant around the corner from both of our homes. The bar was no more than a quarter mile from my house. This place was a historic biker bar. The restaurant had been remodeled into a family-style eatery. Dominic started bartending there to keep the flow of additional money in his pocket.

One day he randomly called me to talk about his new bartending job. He said there were some local troublemakers who came in from time to time, causing problems. He told me, "Soon the return of the Sandman may be necessary."

I laughed and said, "I'm retired, and my wife would kill me if went back to bouncing."

He said, "This place is going to need someone real soon to run security."

"You don't have security?"

Dominic said, "Nope!" The owner didn't think that his restaurant needed a doorman.

Here I was, thinking that I was done working at night, but I was noticeably bored with my newfound freedom, and it would make it easier to pay for graduate school. Plus, I missed having cash in my pocket. At times, I went online looking for part-time jobs, but nothing was as profitable as bouncing. I was always trying to figure out a way to avoid going back to the nightlife, but I was unable to find a comparable option.

The inevitable occurred, and Dominic called me and attempted to sell me on a potential job opportunity at his current part-time gig. Dominic's call did not start with a job offer. It started with a story about the bar that would bring me out of retirement. Like most bar incidents, it began with a couple guys having one too many cocktails. A disagreement ensued, and the verbal banter quickly escalated to a physical altercation. Imagine Dominic working behind the bar with three young, tight-bodied females and not another male staff member in sight. There were a few guys in the kitchen, but no one that could come out and solve a problem like this.

The arguing patrons were a few local hoods. The leader's name was Captain or Cap for short. He had a three-hundred-pound follower who had the largest head I have ever seen that was not on the side of a mountain. I can't remember his name, but for now, let's just call him Jack. On this night, Cap and Jack were in the bar and started arguing with some other young locals. The argument escalated, and tempers hit their apex. They headed outside and were standing nose to nose. The argument quickly turned into a fight among about six men.

Dominic was forced to call the local authorities. He watched the dust fly while on the phone. He described guys bleeding and fighting on top of cars in the parking lot. The police came, and they all dispersed.

The owner heard the story and told Dominic to ask me to come in and work. At first I told my wife that I was just going to talk with the owner. She was beyond furious with the idea.

She said, "You have a family and career. Are you crazy? Don't you remember the twelve staples? Maybe you should look in the mirror at that canyon on the top of your head from that barstool!"

I told her, "We can use the money to pay for my graduate degree and save for our dream home."

She did not care what I said, and I didn't care what she said. Andrea was also frustrated being a project manager at the bank because she didn't think her job was fulfilling. She was considering changing careers and becoming a nurse. We could use the money to finance both of our educations. I called up Burt from the old club to come in and help me handle the locals. He was always looking to make a few dollars. My first night, I came to the bar early to talk with the manager. Her name was Lauren. She was a feisty woman with a loving husband and two kids. She had an amazing personality, always upbeat and willing to explore entertainment options to bring people into the bar.

We became friends quickly. We went to each other's kids' birthday parties. We had couples' nights out to explore restaurants with amazing food. She would do anything for me, and I would do the same for her. She was the only reason my wife stopped complaining about me working at the bar, even though she still hated it.

Lauren's personality was so infectious that a couple of African regulars used to flirt with her to no end. One of them asked to take her to his home country as one of his wives. She said, "I'm married!"

He replied, "So am I," and laughed. Then he said, "Your husband can come, too."

I missed those guys and regulars like that when I wasn't working.

On the first night, Burt and I noticed how obvious it was that the bar was lacking diversity. The locals seemed to have an issue with some minorities. We could tell by the way they described nonwhites while they were talking at the bar. They would say things like, "This country needs to send all of the Mexicans, Muslims, and Guatemalans back to where they came from." They loved to say, "They are taking all of our jobs." I thought it was crazy for them to say things like that, but I was used to it because the bar scene was an unfiltered environment.

During my first night, a local troublemaker was at the bar. He assumed that we were like everyone else in this small town. He had no idea what he was getting into by being disrespectful to us. He tried to start a fight and dared anyone to get in his way.

I walked over, calm and relaxed. I said, "Sir, I believe that it's time for you to vacate the premises."

He simply said, "Whatever," then proceeded to stand in that very spot.

Without hesitation, Burt and I did something that this small town was not used to. I grabbed the guy in the head and neck area. He quickly tried to get out of the choke hold, and all his squirming just made it tighter. Then he started to turn blue while Burt opened the door, and I tossed him into the parking lot. He immediately got up and considered doing something, but of course, he did nothing. He cursed and said he would never come back. I didn't care. I knew by morning, the story about the new angry guy who worked the door would be told. I soon found out that I was right.

A week later, the story had grown into a more violent and charismatic tale. That was exactly what I wanted. The locals coming into the bar immediately started to be more respectful. Of course, this did not last, and eventually Cap and Jack came into the bar and started their shenanigans. Cap was smart and realized quickly that I didn't care about being liked. I just want to get paid without incident.

Jack, on the other hand, would drink and push my buttons. At the end of one of my first nights, he attempted to threaten me. We were standing at the doorway of the establishment, and I looked at him and said, "Be careful what you ask for. I'll give it to you."

He raised his hands and said, "Let's go!"

Without hesitation I took two steps toward him, and I was ready for war. He immediately put his hands up with his palms facing me and said, "Relax! It's not that serious!"

That translates to, "I am a three-hundred-pound coward." He would never fight anyone who really had no fear about getting hit or hitting someone else. He was just one of those guys who used his size to intimidate, but when challenged by a strong-willed individual, he looked for a way out.

Burt and I quickly established ourselves as staples in the bar and as people you should not challenge. We changed the dynamic in the bar and made a new set of friends in the process. At home I never spoke of the bar, and started drinking more and spending more time at the bar after work. I became even more distant around this time because Anthony passed away, making me drift deeper into a slight depression.

## CHAPTER 21
# COMEDY AND SWINGERS

It was 2010, and many years had passed. I realized I had worked security for more than a decade of my life. I paid for college with club money and met my wife through bar connections, and it would possibly ruin my marriage if I let it. When I reflect on my experiences, I remember working security for strippers, musicians, and even a porn star, but this bar exposed me to working security for comedians. This is when I met Brandon. Brandon was a comedian and DJ from Wilmington. He created the opportunity to have comedy events at the bar after encountering someone from the bar at one of his shows. He first started to DJ a few nights a week, and the comedy shows came soon after.

In the beginning, we did not realize how good a comedian he was because he worked the door with us when we were short on staff. Then on other nights, he would DJ. We really did not see his full talent until the shows started. He was amazing when he performed. Brandon had lots of connections in the world of comedy. He sold the bar on having comedy events every few months. Brandon would have comics that were just starting to perform first. He would act as the master of ceremonies, and a headliner that a lot of people knew later on. He had connections to get comedians that were on world-famous radio shows, had famous fathers, and were even in movies. It was so fun to get paid checking IDs and watching the comedians perform.

Most nights I walked into the bar at 9:00 p.m. to start my shift. I worked the door for about an hour until the second bouncer came in at 10:00 p.m. This was also about the time that Brandon would come in and start setting up his DJ equipment. I would go over and talk to him about sports while he was setting up. This one night while we were talking, I looked across the restaurant and saw Layla walking toward the bar. She was probably going to talk to Dominic. They had stayed in touch via social media, but I never was into that. I was a loner and never really wanted to be found, so social media outlets were not for me. Plus, Dominic would keep me in the know about what our friends were doing.

The last thing I had heard about Layla was that she was happily married to a seven-foot basketball player who had been in college at the same time I was. They even had a beautiful little girl. I like her dating him even less than I liked her dating Andre. I started walking over to talk to her, but the manager intercepted me. He needed my help setting up the bar for a special party. About halfway through setting up, I walked over, and Layla seemed to be upset. Dominic told me that he would tell me later so I could finish helping the manager.

I did not know what kind of party we were setting up for, but I guessed that it was nothing big because at around

10:00 p.m., we always cleared the tables from the floor to provide some space for dancing. I noticed that Layla was leaving, and I tried to get her attention, but it was too late.

As she left, I noticed the guy who owned the mom-and-pop hardware store in town walking in with his wife. Their names were Clare and Cliff. Soon after, Janette and Paul arrived. They were a dynamic real-estate couple. The four of them were huddled up at the bar, drinking and talking. I was curious and asked the manager if this was the party. He said, "Yup, that's them." I was relieved because sometimes these parties were for some unrefined individuals, the kind of people who think that they can pop bottles like they won the championship and then realize they don't have enough money to put gas in the car to go home.

Before I knew it, the place was swarming with middle-aged couples. Of course, I did not mind because this meant an easy night of people watching and cleanup before I got paid. As the night progressed, I was sitting next to Brandon in the DJ area, and I realized that these couples were friendly. They were dancing in a group at first. Then the ladies were dancing together, and soon the ladies were dancing with the husbands of other women. At first, I didn't think much of it until a random single guy showed up and all the women greeted him. This made me curious about the dynamics within this group of people.

Later that night, Clare and Janette came over to Brandon to request a song. Brandon played their request, and they start dancing, facing each other like women do. Then they got a little closer and started grinding. I mean, picture two middle-aged married women with their legs interlocked and grinding on each other. I looked at Brandon, and he was at a loss for words. What comedian is ever at a loss for words?

Before I had a chance to blink, they leaned into each other and exchanged a peck on the lips. Brandon patted me on the shoulder and said, "Look at Cliff and Paul." These guys were standing on the sidelines with their drinks in hand, watching all of this take place. Then the random single guy joined their wives dancing and started spanking Claire on the ass. This guy was sandwiched between these two married women. Their husbands just smiled while they watched.

Brandon and I were confused until Paul came over and stood by me. I asked Paul, "What kind of party is this?"

He said, "Don't tell anyone, but this is our swingers group."

I repeated, "Swingers?"

Paul explained that he liked to watch his wife with other women. He said, "I love to watch her get off with a woman."

At this point, I was intrigued. He didn't partake in the festivities, but on these nights, his wife was free to explore being with other women like Janette.

Now, this is where it got complicated. Clare and Janette were girlfriends, and Janette and this single guy were girlfriend and boyfriend. I had to ask Paul just how this night was going to play out, but he had no idea. In Paul's perfect world, Clare and Janette would spend the night together, and Paul would get to watch them. Paul explained that unfortunately Clare and Cliff would probably snatch up the single guy. I wondered, of course, what that meant. Would they have a threesome, or would Janette be taken by the strapping young buck while Paul watched things that he could never do happen to his wife?

The night quickly came to an end, and I watched Clare and Cliff leave with the young guy. Janette and Paul had made a new female friend for the evening. At this point, I assumed the spontaneous weird moments were over. I was wrong. While we were cleaning up, we found a swinger's business card. It was Jeanette's! I knew it was hers because her name, phone number, and e-mail address were on it. Also, it pictured her in a lacy ensemble with her knees separated, showing more than we would ever need to see. There was even a website on the bottom.

Of course, the staff and I had to get on the computer to see what this site was all about. We had no idea that this website was a gateway to an underworld of swingers. They had vacation deals that included hotels, airfare, and the opportunity to meet up with other couples. This site was like a dating site for couples that offered more than you could imagine. We had no idea that anything like this even existed. It was crazy!

Once we had cleaned up and began drinking after work, like we always did, I talked to Dominic about Layla. He said, "Layla just confirmed that her husband has been cheating, and she is getting a divorce."

I was shocked. This couldn't be true. However, I had assumed he would do something like this. I knew for a fact that he had been seen out, spending Layla's money in other bars. Dominic said that she was devastated but willing to kick his ass out without looking back. I was amazed that she did just that. I admired her for being so strong and embracing the challenges of being a single mother with a career. I doubted child support was an option because he didn't have shit. She'd brought everything to the table in this relationship.

On many nights, Dominic and I went over to the younger bartender's house to drink for free. All these kids did was drink after work. It reminded Dominic and me of what it was like when we were young and working in the club. What a crazy night! We laughed about the swingers and got inebriated. Dominic and I got in trouble with our wives for coming home at 4:00 a.m. to watch television and cook a couple of steaks.

## CHAPTER 22
# THE REFRIGERATOR

Like always, it was inevitable that staff turnover would occur. I had lost Burt. He could not continue to work at the bar with me because he had to get up at the crack of dawn to drive his truck for work. Soon it would be me and some pretty good support staff. I had taken the job of running the security staff and checking IDs. I also was the bearer of bad news when people did not follow directions.

One special night, there was an influx of new faces. That is never good for a small-town watering hole. It started with the manager from another drinking establishment. He was so arrogant and felt superior because he managed a bar. This night he had too much to drink, and his reputation of being a troublemaker was resurrected. He felt invincible because he was a large man.

I was at the bar talking to Dominic, and I noticed our new staff member telling this guy that he needed to leave the bar. The guy was basically refusing to leave. At this point, I had newborn little boy at home, and I had worked a very long day with very little sleep. I took a deep breath and slowly walked over. I was not in the mood, and Dominic was sure that this might be the first time that this place saw Sandman!

As I walked over, a patron told Dominic to go get me before I got hurt trying to get this guy out of the bar. Dominic laughed and said, "You have no idea what's about to happen, do you?"

The guy told Dominic, "You don't know who your boy is walking up to, do you?"

Dominic replied, "You don't know the new door guy."

They watched as I approached the situation. Dominic came from behind the bar. The patron told Dominic, "You better go get your boy before he gets hurt."

Dominic said, "I'm going over there to save your homeboy, not mine."

I told the gentleman it was time to leave. He ignored me. I walked over and picked him up into the air like a small child. I tossed him into the hostess stand in the front of the bar. It broke into several pieces. I grabbed him, picked him up off the floor by his face, and launched him out of the front door. Then I said, "Have a good night."

The other doorman stood at the door in amazement. The guy got up off the pavement and started yelling at him. I turned around and asked, "Are you talking to me?"

He immediately said, "No! I'm talking to the other guy."

I went back into the bar and fixed the hostess stand. Then I took a seat, and I started checking IDs for a wedding party.

Soon, Dominic came over and said, "There is a guy in that wedding party you just let in who is not allowed in the bar." He explained that a few weeks ago, on a night I was off, he was being belligerent and was asked to leave. Lauren was managing, and he called her names that I would never say to any women. That did not sit well with me for two reasons. First, she was a woman, and no real man talks to a woman like that. Second, she was my friend, and there was no way I would pass up the opportunity to let karma work through my hands.

Now he was in the bar with his friends and family after a wedding. We walked over and told his brother that he needed to leave immediately. A few minutes passed, and he was still in the bar. We walked over to his parents and told them that he needed to leave. They proceeded to talk to him, and a few minutes later, he was still at the bar. The family then pleaded with Lauren to forget about how disrespectful he was. She told them, "He must leave before the guy at the door makes him leave."

Then one of the female bartenders came over to me and said, "The guy that's banned just said that you guys are going to have to throw him out."

I told her, "The customer is always right, and we must oblige him by respecting his wishes."

We walked over to him and told him it was time to go. He leaned over the bar and glanced over his right shoulder at us. Then he just turned his back to us and faced the bar with his drink in hand. I looked at one bouncer and gave him the nod to get him out. He grabbed the guy with both hands. Then the bouncer, Dominic, and I grabbed him from different sides and dragged him toward the kitchen door. I directed them this way because it was an easier exit than the front door. As we were going through the kitchen, he squirmed, and we accidently on purpose ran his head directly into the refrigerator. We got him outside, and he dropped to his knees on the pavement in the alley. He was angry and disoriented. He stumbled away toward the parking lot to go home.

His brother came around the corner and started yelling at Dominic. He called Dominic an asshole and said all of that was unnecessary because we should have let him stay. I intervened immediately on Dominic's behalf and said, "This is your fucking fault. If you'd got him to leave, none of this would have happened. You knew he was not allowed in, and you let him come in anyway."

He quickly walked away and took his brother. Amazingly, many at the party stayed in the bar and apologized for his behavior. The crazy thing is that they let him drive himself to the emergency room and stayed in the bar drinking. They must have been a real close-knit family...*not!* The family told us he had a drinking problem. Soon afterward, I was told the incident provoked a family intervention. He went to a facility to treat his alcohol addiction and sobered up. Months later, he came in and apologized for his behavior. As terrible as it was for him to have been thrown out in such a violent way, it was beneficial for him to grow into a better man. God works in mysterious ways.

That night I met a guy who rode a Harley-Davidson. He was at the bar and loved how I handled people. He asked me if I would work a bike event as security for him. He was a manager at a motorcycle shop, and they were having a large bike rally with live bands, radio personalities, and lots of venders. This event was outside and covered several acres of land. There were thousands of motorcycle enthusiasts there for the event. I met lots of celebrities that day. That was the last major event that I worked. That biker and I became close friends.

## CHAPTER 23
# EXIT PLAN

I had just gotten to work, and I was thirsty. I went over to Dominic to get a drink. On my way over to the bar, I saw one of my favorite regulars. That night she gave me a great big hug and told me about this terrible date she'd gone on that very night. She was a full-figured woman, and boy, did she have a story for me.

She explained how she had met up with an old school friend, and he asked her out to dinner and a movie. They went to the movie, and while at dinner, they started talking about sex. He told her how he had a small penis and could never satisfy her. She told me that she just sat in her seat and ate her food. He didn't take the hint and continued to explain how he understood that a big girl like her needed a well-hung man. He continued to discuss his physical limits but tried to sell her on his ability to pleasure her orally. He then went on to explain that he could spell the alphabet with his tongue and that he spoke Spanish. He told her that she would love his rolling *r*'s. She said he promised to speak the Latin language of love in her nether regions.

Once she had finished eating and he had paid the bill, she immediately gave him an excuse to leave. She was not sure about this guy and met him out at the movie and the restaurant. Driving herself worked well because she left him and came straight to the bar. We told the story to Dominic and still to this day, whenever I see her, we talk about that night.

This night was off to a fun start, but it turned into something entirely different. It led to another incident with a drunk patron that had the police asking me to pick him out of a police lineup and going to court. This incompetent fool took a beer mug into the parking lot, and my favorite female manager of all time simply asked him to give it back. He put the mug behind his back and said, "I don't know what you're talking about."

I walked over and said, "Either give it back or I will just take it from you."

He told me, "Don't make me pop my trunk and get my gun."

How could he say that with only a flimsy gate separating us? I stepped close to him so that he was within arm's reach. I smiled and said, "What makes you think you're going to make it to your car?"

The blood disappeared from his face, leaving him as pale as a ghost. During this time, I had hired a bouncer friend who had gone to jail for murder. He had tattoos all over him. He had a hand with the middle finger up tattooed on his bicep. He reached over and took the mug from the startled, barely legal idiot.

Suddenly, a car pulled up with a girl driving. It was his girlfriend coming to save the day. He got in, and they left. Then while we were in the bar about to clear the patrons out, we saw our small meat smoker that sat outside the kitchen door thrown at the bar's front door. We saw him standing there, and he saw us and started running. My friend with the documented violent history took the chance to chase him down and ran after him. Now, my friend is a big man weighing about 265 pounds and with about 5 percent body fat. He caught the kid and simply tapped him on the shoulder. He sent a clear message that he could have hurt him if that was his intention.

Months later, we would go to court and simply request to ban him from the establishment. He agreed. Then he told the court that he was afraid of me and wanted a no-contact order against me. I laughed and soon found out that I knew his cousin. His cousin told him that he was lucky we didn't hurt him that night. I guess that frightened him.

After court, I started considering retirement again. I had finally had enough after twelve years of being affiliated with the night scene. It was time for me to go. I immediately started saving money for my exit. My plan was to surprise Andrea when I came home from my last night and tell her I was finally finished.

## CHAPTER 24

# THE SANDMAN MUST BE DEAD

It was 10:00 p.m., and I was steadily checking IDs at the door. I was waiting for the other two bouncers to come to work. These guys were as unique as anyone I had ever worked with. One was a mailman, and the other was a young college wrestler. The mailman was a big man, weighing 270 pounds and standing about six foot one. The wrestler was about the same height, but he tipped the scales at around three hundred pounds with the agility of a much smaller man. I looked out of the front door to view their arrival in the parking lot. I couldn't wait for them to get here so I could pass off the door duties to one of them and then go off and sit in the corner of the bar on the stage to pass the time. Then off in the distance, I saw one familiar vehicle barreling down the road and swiftly turning into the parking lot. Then came a second. Finally, they were here.

Before my additional staff could get out of their cars, about five guys walked through the parking lot. I knew them well. It was Cap and Jack with a few of their degenerate associates. They looked like what they were: trouble. They came to the door, and Cap and Jack spoke to me and introduced one of the padres. They explained that he'd just gotten home from prison. I hated the guys who would come out to the bar on their first night out, trying to live the dreams that they had conjured up while incarcerated. They usually got drunk and seemed to do everything possible to land back in prison. We talked for a second or two before all the guys except Jack went inside.

Jack proceeded to tell me that it was his birthday and that they might have a few other guys coming out. I simply said, "I am tired, and I am not in the mood for BS."

Of course, Jack was quick to tell me how it was all love.

I watched Jack go inside and wondered what kind of trouble I would have to deal with tonight. I turned around to the front door, and there were the mailman and the wrestler. I looked at them and said, "One of you take the door, and the other work the floor for glasses."

I moved to my chill-out corner of the stage to sit and watch this group of idiots take shot after shot. I also noticed them going into the unisex bathroom in a rotation. We had talked to them in the past about using a framed decorative mirror hanging on the bathroom wall to snort cocaine. We had noticed it months ago, at the end of a long night when we were cleaning up. We saw the residue between the streaks on the mirror left from the cocaine. I assumed that it just might be one of those nights.

I heard a knock on the door behind the stage. It was my favorite DJ. I let him in so he could set up his equipment. I moved the two tables together so he could put his turntables and mixer on them. Then I heard lurid banter coming from the bar. I knew it was Cap and friends. We watched, but still they had done nothing to cause a real concern. I did take a moment to walk over and say that they need to lower their voices. I also suggested that slowing down on the shots couldn't hurt. They just laughed and hugged. I went behind the bar and told the bartenders to monitor how much they were drinking and how fast. They knew to tell me immediately if someone had too much and needed to leave.

Time passed, and it was getting close to the end of the night. I was thinking that we made it through another night. I was wrong. Lauren came to tell me that Jack was outside in the smoking area acting up, but I should just keep an eye on him. I went outside, and by then, all of them were smoking cigarettes and, of course, drinking. A gate enclosed the smoking area. The rule was that we did not jump over the gate. We made the rule to stop people from jumping over the gate to avoid being carded at the front door and to evade paying a cover and to keep those who were exiting that way from skipping out on a tab.

As soon as I came out, the felon in their group jumped over the gate to walk out to his car in the parking lot. He stumbled and almost fell when he hit the pavement. I walked over and told them that he couldn't do that. They said they would take care of him, and he wouldn't do it again.

Of course, he came back from the car and jumped over the gate instead of walking around it. I told him, "Don't ever do that again."

He said, "Or what?"

I glared at Cap and Jack, and they took him inside the bar. As they escorted him inside, he looked back at me like he was invincible. I had a difficult time letting those moments pass. With age comes wisdom, and I knew it was better to let those moments go, but about five short years ago, I would have tried to snap him in half.

Dominic joked with me and said, "The Sandman must be dead because the dude I know would never let anyone disrespect him." He was always implying that I was getting soft. That was never the case. I was smart enough to realize that, as a husband, father, and career-driven man working on my master's, this was beneath me. I had to look at the bigger picture.

At around 12:45 a.m., we would make the last call for drinks and close the smoking section. I was about to do this when Lauren ran out to bring me inside. The mailman squared off with Jack. I was so tired and could think only about my bed. I did not feel like dealing with this tonight or really any other night. I said, "I don't know what's going on, but the night is almost over, so just go home."

Jack said, "Let's do it!"

The mailman looked in my direction for the green light to physically remove him. I hesitated for a second because I knew the rest of their party would soon come over to make things worse. After a deep breath, I told the mailman, "Move furniture!"

The look on Jack's face was priceless. The table was flipped, and the mailman grabbed Jack and tossed him out of the front door.

## The Other Side of the Velvet Rope

Then from behind us came the rest of the crew, led by the newly freed felon. I grabbed him and tossed him over the gate. I made sure he landed flat on his back in the parking lot. He was in pain with a matching pair of deflated lungs. I started asking them to leave. Cap started cursing and telling us that he was tired of being treated like this because he spent money in this bar. I always told guys that we didn't need them in the bar. If it was that bad here, go someplace else. They could go anyplace in the world, but they wanted to fight to come in this hole-in-the-wall bar. I never understood this kind of mind-set. I always said if your pockets are that deep, go to Vegas or New York or leave the country and go to Europe.

We were all in front of the bar outside, yelling back and forth. Then we saw a car pull into the parking lot, speeding and cutting corners like a race car. Three guys jumped out to back up Cap and Jack. The staff and I had our backs to the door. They were pushing forward and threatening to shoot the bar up. One got in my face, yelling. I calmly said, "You have seconds to back up out of my face."

With me being the smallest, I guessed he assumed I would be intimidated. I was getting agitated. I snapped and grabbed him by the throat. I picked him up off the ground and tossed him into the parking lot. He landed on his back, hard. I looked all of them in their eyes. They were all scared.

It was silent before Cap started screaming about being a victim. I threw my hands up and said, "Whatever, I am going inside to clean." I was afraid that I might become enraged and really try to hurt someone.

The yelling went on for about fifteen minutes, and I just stayed inside. I heard Cap's friends threatening my life and everyone else's from inside the bar. I knew that I had too much to lose to continue working in this environment. I needed quit as soon as I could for my sanity and my marriage. It was the time of hour when it is later than night but earlier than morning. I got a text from Rush saying, "Call me ASAP. I know you're up because I know you're working."

## CHAPTER 25
# THE CONVERSATION

I called, and the first words I uttered were, "Rush, what's going on?"

Rush sighed and said, "So much has happened in the past few days. Abdulla is in the hospital, and it looks like he doesn't have long to live."

I asked, "Was he in an accident or something?"

He said, "Just go see him as soon as possible because he may not have long to live."

I took the information that Rush had given me, and I went to the hospital to see Abdulla the very next day. Throughout the night before, during the drive, and at that moment when I arrived at the hospital parking lot, I kept asking myself, *Is Abdulla going to die, too?*

I walked into the hospital and went to the floor that he was on. I got to the nurse's desk to find out what room he was in, and before the nurse could answer, a female voice said, "You must be the Sandman." I looked over to see a woman I had never encountered before. She had the most beautiful smile, and as she walked toward me, her eyes filled with water. The flood gates were about to open when she stretched out her arms and hugged me so tight. She whispered to me in her emotionally cracking voice, "He said to us that he will not leave this place before seeing you one last time." She kissed me on the cheek and introduced me to Abdulla's children, aunts, uncles, and the mothers of his children that I did not know. Then she said, "Forgive me for my poor manners. I am Yvette, his high school sweetheart. Please go in and see him."

I walked into the hospital room, and Abdulla was lying down with eyes closed, facing the window with a chair next to it for visitors. The 240-pound man I had grown to know was emaciated. It had been a couple of years since I had seen him at one of our college homecomings. I stepped slowly and quietly so as not to wake him if he were sleep.

Then Abdulla's weak voice said, "Can you see him?"

I said, "See who or what?"

He said, "The devil. The vices associated with my promiscuity have forced Allah to send him for me. He sits in that chair every day and keeps checking his watch. Soon he will check the time, stand up, and reach out his hand to take me out of here." Abdulla started coughing and whispered, "Water."

His hand arose from beneath the sheet to the bedside table. He looked exhausted from just talking to me. I was still standing a ways away from his bed. I was taking in all of the instruments and devices that were connected to him. The beeping was driving me crazy. I took a few steps closer, and his head turned away from his view of the devil, and he smiled at me. I took a few more steps and grabbed the glass of water. He leaned forward, and I put the glass to his lips.

I began to feel more comfortable, and I asked him, "What happened?"

He said, "Infidelity. I have beautiful children I will never see become adults because I am dying from AIDS."

"What? It must be something else."

Abdulla smiled. "It's OK. I've known for a while."

I refused to ask any other questions. I pulled the chair closer to his bedside. I put my hand on his arm, and we talked. I explained to him that my wife hated me working in the club, and he used his situation to explain how the present is a gift.

He said, "If you do not embrace what is available now, it will soon become the past, and the opportunity to be a husband and father may cease to exist as you know it at this moment." We talked for a couple hours while the nurses came in and out of the room to make sure he was comfortable.

The last thing I said to him was, "I will see you soon." I felt horrible saying that. I knew they were preparing him to be moved to a hospice facility. There was very little chance of me seeing him alive again. I never saw him again. As I left the room and closed the door, I saw Billy. We had a very serious conversation.

Billy said, "It's a shame what he is going through. That's why after getting caught in the club that night by my old girlfriend and new girlfriend, I knew it was time to stop the games."

I was amazed at his conviction. Between Billy's and Abdulla's sentiments about their misogynistic treatment of women in the past, I needed to take care of a good women who just wanted me to leave the club before someone did more than just hit me over the head with a barstool.

## CHAPTER 26
# THE DEATH OF A PATRON

My last night in the bar turned out to be bittersweet. As usual, when I left for work, Andrea was quiet and had her blood pressure going through the roof because I was still working at night. She worried herself to death that something bad would happen to me. She had no idea that this was my last night. Being so close to the end of my time at the bar, felt freeing, but my last night was haunted by the death of a patron. I felt like death was always around me. We had let a young man leave too drunk to drive a few weeks ago because we had been too preoccupied with Cap and Jack. This young man crashed his car into a pole on his way home. He was thrown from the vehicle and bled to death quickly.

On the day of his funeral, his mother and friends came into the bar to celebrate his life. I was there that night, and I had the opportunity to speak with his mother. I never mentioned that I was working the night her son died, but I did tell her that I knew him as a regular.

With tears in her eyes, she said, "My son loved this bar, and I felt it was only right for us to come here after his funeral." She started crying and gave me a hug. She wrapped her arms around me tightly. It was as if she felt like a part of her child was within the bar and she was thankful for us being a part of so many happy memories for her baby boy.

At the end of the night, I always talked to Dominic, and he told me what was going on with our friends on social media. I hated social media and never wanted to be found. I thought that if we were good enough friends, you could always just call me. Tonight's discussion would be our last one in the bar after a long night. He told me that Mookie, his childhood friend, had drowned at sea. He went out on a boat with two other guys and the boat capsized. I was shocked.

I asked, "Is everyone OK?"

He said, "Mookie drowned."

"Did anyone else drown?"

Dominic said, "He was the only casualty."

I immediately thought back to my time at the bar and realized that death or prison were the common endings for a person in his line of work. I could still hear the conversation between the freckle-faced girl and him at the bar the last night I saw them both. She had still been scarred after almost overdosing on the drugs he gave her.

Even though we talked and reminisced like we always did, I still did not say anything about retiring. No one but me knew this would be my last night at the bar. I'd had enough, and I wanted to finish my master's degree, pursue my doctorate, and one day run my own education program. But first, I needed to get through my last night and clean up around the bar.

## CHAPTER 27
# THE END AS I SEE IT

The night ended, and we wiped down the tables and moved the chairs for the floors to be mopped. I was emotional, but most of the staff just assumed I was tired. It was hard to come to grips with the idea of it being over. My friends were dying one by one, and I knew the ego boost of the nightlife would be gone as well. Then I started thinking of how much free time I would have to spend with my family. No more arguments about me working at night. We would be able to take vacations because I wouldn't be working during the weekend. I would have time to finish school and take a break before starting my doctorate. I thought about these things while we straightened up the bar before I was paid one last time.

I was excited to go home and wake my wife up to say it was finally over and I was done. I would miss the extra money, but it would be fine because we both made good livings. I finally felt free because I was down to only one job for the first time since I started working in college.

I walked through the door of our home, and I couldn't wait to tell Andrea that I was finally done. I walked into our bedroom and tried not to startle her because she was usually asleep when I arrived home. I quietly walked to her side of the bed and tapped her on her shoulder to wake her. She was unresponsive. I shook her, and she looked like she had possibly had a stroke. I called 911 and grabbed our baby boy from his crib. The ambulance came and took her straight to the emergency room.

My son and I sat outside, waiting to hear from the doctor. I didn't call anyone. At the time, I did not feel I had too many friends to call. Anthony was dead, Abdulla was dead, and now my wife might soon be gone as well. I just held my son in my arms and waited. The doctor came out and explained that Andrea had a cerebral aneurysm. It was a common condition for women between the ages of thirty-five and sixty. She'd had no warning signs and had seemed to be completely healthy. The doctor went on to explain that most aneurysms do not burst, but hers must have around the time I arrived home. He asked if she was upset because these things were triggered from a rise in blood pressure. I told him that she was upset every night I worked. The doctor explained that she would not have long to live, and at that point, I was speechless and just stared at the floor.

I was devastated. I reflected on how much of my time had been spent working to make more money to pay for more things and how I had wasted valuable time that could have been spent with my family. I was a liar. I'd promised myself that when Anthony died, I would spend more time with the people I loved. If I had made good on my promise when he passed away, I would not have been in this predicament. I knew now what was important in life, and I should not have spent so much of my time chasing a dollar because no matter how many I obtained, it was still never enough.

I fulfilled my promises that I had made to myself and that I was going to make to her before she passed. I finished my master's and my doctorate before Dominic could finish his master's. I became a school leader, and I am the administrator of one of the best education programs in the state of Delaware. I saved my money and bought the dream house that Andrea and I always wanted. Just as I had promised her.

These tragedies also cemented the respect of my father. He was and still is so proud of how I was able to find my own path in life. Everything I did to become successful was done in an unconventional way. He respected how I was could be around the chaos of the club but never became consumed with the aspects of the club that could bring despair. He told me he could never imagine being so proud to watch me prosper after losing so many people to death's wrath. His approval was always my driving force.

# EPILOGUE

The club is a building with flashing lights and loud music. For many, the club is like that moment in time when you pass a car accident and can see the lights from the first responders and everyone looks to see what happened but no one wants to see anything horrific. That's what it was like at times in the club.

For me, the club was a way to make money, build friendships, and support the ego I had lost when I stopped playing football in college. I used the club as financial and emotional support. I was never dependent on the club monetarily, but I loved the money I could make in a night. Money was the vice that brought me into the club every night. Emotionally, all the staff were in the same boat, just trying to get by and make a few dollars to make life easier. This built camaraderie among us.

Vices are what bring people to the club. If you are an alcoholic, that vice will be embraced at the club—especially by the club owner and bar staff if you pay your tab. Of course, if you leave a little extra for the preparer of the drink, you will increase your chances of keeping the attention of the bartender for the night. Others come to the club looking for sex. The men and women make sexual advances that could never take place in any venue other than the club. It was hard to watch women who had told me on a bad drunken night how they were victims of sexual and physical abuse as children become dependent on giving their bodies to others to feel love.

Then there are those who literally prey on the weak—the pimps and the drug pushers. They spend their nights looking for the emotionally damaged to provide them with some form of toxin to help them cope with life's emotional turbulence. They sell them false dreams of a better life.

Working in the club helped me understand how hard life can be for all of us. All those at the club, staff or patrons, were there looking for something that the club could not truly provide. We were all just looking for something. We did not know what it was or even what to do if we found it.

The truth is the club is just a building—a building that will be whatever the people inside make it. It could be a place filled with drugs and degradation, or it could be a place where many find peace. Regardless, the club is a microcosm of the world. Just like the club, the world is a place we can make our own.

I was so busy worrying about what was going on in the club that I forgot about the world outside it. During my time in the club, I lost friends, family, and my wife. It took that for me to focus more on the world outside the club. Remember: everything is fine in moderation, but at the moment when it consumes you, you should take a step back and evaluate what is really important on the other side of the velvet rope.

# ABOUT THE AUTHOR

Dwight BoNey has drawn upon his own personal experiences as a former bouncer, bartender, and security manager. He spent a decade in the club industry before quitting to pursue a new career.

Made in United States
North Haven, CT
23 July 2024